The Eridanos Library 13

Juan García Ponce

Encounters

Translated by Helen Lane
Introduction by Octavio Paz

Eridanos Press

Original Spanish title *Encuentros*

"The Cat," "The Square," and "The Seagull" first
published as *Encuentros* by Fondo de Cultura Económica,
Mexico City 1972. "Anticipation" first published in
Figuraciones by Fondo de Cultura Económica,
Mexico City 1982.

Distributed in the U.S.A. by Rizzoli International
Publications, Inc., 597 Fifth Avenue, New York, NY 10017

Cloth: ISBN 0941419-25-8
Paper: ISBN 0941419-24-X
LC 88-83030

Contents

Introduction

by Octavio Paz

The corpus of works by Juan García Ponce is one of the vastest in contemporary Mexican literature. It is also one of the most varied: novels, short stories, drama, essays, literary, and art criticism. To this diversity of genres must be added that of the territories he explores: eroticism and intellectual argument, art criticism and metaphysics, literary speculation and moral reflection, naturalistic descriptions and reticences that say without saying, linear and symbolic narrative. García Ponce has written, generously and intelligently, about the painters and writers of his generation; he has also devoted penetrating studies to figures as different as Robert Musil and Pierre Klossowski, José Lezama Lima and José Bianco. His critical thought, his discoveries and his enthusiasms, his positive and negative judgments have exerted an influence that has enlivened Mexican literature and art for over twenty years. Yet his many essays are simply peripheral prolongations and reflections of his central field of activity: prose fiction. García Ponce is above all else a storyteller, and his critical works are ancillary to his works of imagination. He is not an essayist who writes novels, but a novelist who writes essays.

Within his prose fiction, his short stories occupy a place apart. Not because they are different in nature from his novels; despite the variety of his forms and experiments, García Ponce's subject is one and is present, either explicitly or implicitly, in all his narratives. The difference between novel and short story in his work is not one of substance; his short stories say the same thing as his novels, but in another voice and with another intonation. They are bends in a river where the impetuous current seems to grow calmer; without ceasing to flow, it murmurs in a quieter, slower voice. For an instant the vortex becomes motionless and then, suddenly limpid, the prose falls silent: a confidence shared without words. In all of García Ponce's stories we are present at the gradual unveiling of a secret, but once they arrive at the very brink of revelation, they hang back: the nucleus, the essential truth, is what is *not* said. As I write this, I am thinking above all of the little book called *Encounters,* first published in 1972 by the Fondo de Cultura Económica and which now Eridanos Press has had the fine idea of publishing in English. It comprises two brief stories, "The Cat" and "The Square," and a longer story, almost a novella, "The Seagull."* The three texts number among García Ponce's best. We may say of them, without exaggera-

*"Anticipation," also included in the present edition, was published ten years later in another short-story collection: *Figuraciones.* (Editor's note)

tion, that they are three *precipitates*, in the chemical sense of the word, of his fictions, his inventions, and his obsessions.

Despite its strange subject, "The Cat" is the story that cleaves most faithfully to García Ponce's usual manner. (Perhaps that is why he later wrote another version of it, longer and more explicit, richer in psychological overtones, but less mysterious.) A couple finds a cat, or rather, the cat finds them. Without self-consciousness, they simply accept the presence of this intruder as they play their erotic games; almost imperceptibly the little creature becomes a talisman; without "the fixed gaze of those half-open yellow eyes on her naked body," the woman is not able to give herself to the man nor does he really desire her. Their passion depends upon a third party: a small animal presence, as enigmatic as desire, which like desire appears out of nowhere and leads them to the unknown. "The Square" also centers on an encounter, not with an emissary from the world of desire, but with time itself. An elderly man searches for time past, his time, in a public square of the provincial city where he has lived all his life; he searches for it as day is ending, at an hour when darkness is descending on the trees and the last passersby are leaving the arcades, but what he finds is an infinite, nameless happiness, a far vaster time, a time that is never gone though it is always going by.

The two experiences, that of the cat—the sign of desire—and that of nightfall in the square—the canceling-out of signs—confronts us with a mystery that has traditionally been the subject of the reflections of philosophers and the substance of the visions of mystics. García Ponce is not a believer, but in his most successful texts there comes a moment when his sensibility makes contact with a magnetic field; it is easier to feel the fascination of such passages than to describe them; it is a sort of religious ecstasy that it would not be inaccurate to call quietistic. In another Mexican writer, José Revueltas, I also note a vein of religiosity, although it has a different and even contrary meaning: Revuelta's Marxist Christianity is active and fulfills itself in sacrifice; García Ponce's religiosity is erotic and aesthetic: *the via contemplativa.*

"The Seagull" is an unusual work, not least because of its subject. It is the story of the meeting of two adolescents at a Mexican seaside beach. Stories about adolescents are not a frequent feature of the various Hispanic literatures. The barrenness and rigidity of our classics have not received the critical notice they deserve: in Spanish novels the typical adolescent is not a Stephen Dedalus, a Grand Meaulnes, a Werther, or a Tom Sawyer but a Lazarillo de Tormes or a Guzmán de Alfarache: an anti-hero, a *pícaro.* The Calisto and Melibea of Fernando de Rojas's *La Celestina* might be the exception, but when they fall in love they are already what society and their breeding have made them; they do not discover themselves when they discover love. The world in which García Ponce's two teenagers move is a world apart, in the social sense: both belong to the upper middle class. The girl, moreover, is a foreigner. The isolation of the two youngsters is not only social but psychological as well. Their passion isolates them from their playmates and, like the cat that intrudes upon the lovers in the first story, that passion leads them to discover a violent and awesome reality: that of their own selves.

xiv

The story is written in a prose that moves along unhurriedly, like the flow of happy days that are all alike, with pools of shadow, sudden bright flashes, and secret vibrations. Light on the sea: a rippling of waves, breasts, backs, bellies, muscles. A world ruled by two senses: touch and sight. Both are the servants of desire. Nature is constantly present, at times as pleasure (seeing and touching, being seen and being caressed) and at others as a terrible enigma (What is there behind forms? What does that gaze conceal?). There is one unforgettable moment: the episode of the two youngsters in the cemetery of the little port town, at the sea's edge, stretched out on the grass, beneath a night sky studded with stars, peeking at the will-o'-the-wisps that suddenly appear above the graves. The two adolescents' desire has something of plant life about it: it grows, ripens, splits open. It is a crystallization, not in Stendhal's sense but in Lawrence's: it is not a sentiment but an instinct, something involving not the head but the blood. The final revelation is instantaneous and terrible: sex is violence, murder, destruction. The children cease to be children as they wallow in the dust soaked with the blood of the seagull that the boy has killed. Is the sexual act inseparable from crime?

There is a word that appears repeatedly in García Ponce's writings: innocence. In nearly all of his novels and short stories, however, innocence is invariably allied to those passions that we call evil or perverse: cruelty, rage, lust, the deliriums of the exasperated imagination, and, finally, the entire range of pleasures that we condemn severely and yet at the same time find fascinating. It is a matter of inclinations that are almost always irresistible, as Racine says in a carefully restrained alexandrine: *quel que soit le penchant qui m'attire* (whatever the attraction may be that draws me to you). How can love be innocent if it is doomed to contain, to a greater or lesser degree, a measure of perversity? Psychoanalysts inform us that even kissing is an oral perversion. The word innocence, however, is not really a moral or scientific term but a religious one: innocence is a fullness of being, just as sin is a lack. Innocence is abundance; sin is want. This Lawrence knew perfectly well, and speaking of his novels in a letter to a friend, he told him that all of them revolved around the enigma of sexuality "and have been written out of the depths of my religious experience."

In García Ponce's case, two other elements must be set alongside religious experience: the act of looking and spectacle. In his novels sight is the sovereign sense, as it was for the philosophers of Antiquity. The eye perceives the essential ambiguity of the universe and discovers in this ambiguity not the duality of the moral realm but the unity of the religious vision: all is one and one is all. Unitive theology or a voyeur's aesthetic? Both. Between the prurient poses of Julio Romano and the spiritual exercises of Saint Catherine of Siena, the narrative becomes by turn a libertine ceremony and a sacred mystery. The theater was one of García Ponce's first passions: he soon abandoned it but it lives on between the covers of his novels. Not only, as might be supposed, because of his use of dialogue, but also because of the way in which certain episodes are constructed: the text becomes a sort of stage rear, and the reader, turned into an onlooker, contemplates, or more exactly, *watches* the action. In certain cases (in the expanded version of "The Cat," for instance), one does not have the impression that one is present at a performance in a theater but, rather, that one is peeping through a keyhole: the "tableaux vivants" of pornography transformed into a ritual of signs that come together and separate to form, literally, figures of a language irreducible to words. Bodies link together like signs, form sentences, and *say*. But what do they say? García Ponce's entire *oeuvre* attempts to answer that question. A desperate question, and perhaps one without an answer: innocence looks at itself; it neither thinks itself nor says itself.

Encounters

. . . a language that expresses itself
in images none of which longs to
be the last one.

Robert Musil:
The Man Without Qualities

The Cat

OBJRCT

The cat appeared one day and from then on was always there. It did not seem to belong to anyone in particular, to any of the apartments, but to the whole building. Even its attitude led one to suppose that it had not chosen the building, making it its own, but rather, that the building had chosen it, so perfectly was its figure superimposed upon the general appearance of the hallways and stairs. That was how D started seeing it, in the late afternoon, as he left his apartment, or at night sometimes, as he returned to it: gray and small, stretched out on the mat outside the door of the apartment halfway down the hall on the second floor. When D, having climbed the first flight of stairs, turned to walk down the hallway, the cat, gray and small, a young cat still, turned its head round toward him, wanting him to look into its eyes, of an odd yellow, burning amid its soft gray fur. Then it half closed them for a moment, till they became a thin slit of yellow light, and turned its head back round, ignoring the gaze of D, who went on looking at it nonetheless, touched by its lonely frailness and a little uncomfortable because of the disquieting weight of its presence. At other times, rather than in the second floor hallway, D would suddenly come across it curled up in one of the corners of the vast lobby or walking along slowly, its body hugging the wall, paying no heed to the warning of strange footsteps approaching. At other times still, it would appear on one of the flights of stairs, twined about the iron balusters, and then it would go down or up the stairs in front of D, starting off without turning round to look at him and getting out of his way just as he was about to overtake it, coiling about the balusters once again, shy and frightened, though once he had gone past, D could feel its yellow gaze on his back.

The building D lived in was an old but well-preserved one, constructed with the sage architecture of thirty or forty years ago which valued and reserved a place for accessory elements, the style of which had become anachronistic owing to its very character and yet had not lost its sober beauty. The downstairs lobby, the stairwell, and the hallways occupied a vast space in the building and set their own solemn, antiquated stamp upon the entire edifice. A few days, perhaps a few weeks before the cat appeared, the unpredictable will of the doormen, as old and imperturbable as the building and all crammed in together with their children and grandchildren in the custodians' cubbyhole on the ground floor, keeping a mistrustful eye on the tenants as they came and went, had removed from the lobby the two heavy, threadbare velvet sofas and the small but solid wooden writing desk whose age-old presence accentuated the singularly conservative character of the building, untouched by the passage of time, and it seemed to D that the cat was now occupying the place of the furniture. In some way or other, its inexplicable presence went well with the tone of the building and, significantly, D never saw it among the large round earthenware containers filled with broad-leaved tropical plants which the young couple in the apartment next to his had taken it upon themselves to place on the stair landings to liven up the hallway. The cat seemed to be averse to this remote reminiscence of a garden; the bare, spare elements of hallways and stairs were his territory. And so, in the same way that he had become accustomed to the two sofas and the writing desk that had filled the empty space of the lobby and now missed their presence, D became accustomed to coming across the cat all of a sudden and receiving its usual indifferent look and to seeing it go down or up the stairs in front of him without wondering who it belonged to.

D lived alone in his apartment and spent in it most of the time not taken up by his easy job, from which, in exchange for a few hours a day of methodical work, he received enough to live on; but his solitude was not total: a girlfriend visited him almost every day and stayed in the apartment every weekend. The two of them got along well together, and it might even be said, if it is of any importance, that they loved each other, although on a plane conditioned and determined by their bodies, which to the two of them, at least, appeared to be satisfactory enough. A pleasure

D never tired of was to look, from almost every angle of the little apartment, in the idle hours that stretched out before them on Sunday mornings, at the naked body of his friend lying indolently on the bed, shifting from one attractive position to yet another that unfailingly accentuated even further a nakedness, which, owing to the awareness on her part that he was admiring her and finding satisfaction in the exposure of her body, was almost insolent. Whenever D was by himself remembering his friend, he imagined her that way, stretched out lazily on the bed, with the bed-clothes that might cover her invariably thrown back even when she was dozing, offering her body for contemplation with a total abandon, as if the one reason for its existence was that D admired it and in reality it did not belong to her but to him and perhaps to the furniture in the room as well and even to the branches of the trees in the street, which could be seen through the windows, and to the sunlight entering through them, radiant and diffuse.

Sometimes her face remained hidden in the pillow and her dark chestnut hair, neither long nor short, almost impersonal in its absence of relationship with her facial features, crowned the long line of her back extending downward till it disappeared in the ample curve of her hips and the firm outline of her buttocks. Farther on were her long legs, parted at an arbitrary angle, yet closely related. At such times her body to D was almost of the nature of an object. But also when she was lying facing him, allowing her tiny breasts with their bright nipples and the magnificent stretch of her belly with no more than a hint of her navel and the dark area of her pubis between her open legs to show, there was something remote and impersonal about her body's deliberate self-abandon and its surrender to contemplation. Beyond question, D knew and loved that body and could not fail to experience the reality of its presence as it came and went from one place to another in the apartment carrying on those little everyday activities whose meaning becomes lost owing to the mechanical way in which we get them over and done with. And he likewise felt it when she undressed in front of him or when it was she who moved, still naked, from one place to another in the apartment, suddenly turning toward D to make a trivial remark. Hence, the presence of his friend, their shared solitude, the deep, calm sensuality of their relationship, in which she was always naked and belonged to him, formed part of his apartment in the same way that it was part of his life and when they were with other people the knowledge of this relationship would suddenly come back to D, involving him with a disturbing force that made him feel for the skin underneath her clothes and separated him from everything while at the same time it made him sense that the knowledge he had of her was projected toward the others as a sort of need to share her secret attraction with them. So to him she was like a bridge that one and all must cross in the same way that the light coming in through the windows fell on her body as she lay stretched out on the bed and the way that the furniture in the apartment seemed to look at her along with him.

On one of those Sunday mornings when she was lying drowsing on the bed, D heard, through the closed door of the apartment, pitiful, insistent meows, rolling back on themselves till they became a single, monotonous sound. D realized, to his surprise, that this was the first time the cat had marked its presence in this way. His apartment was directly above the one in front of the door of which, one floor below, the cat lay on the mat; but the meows seemed to be coming from somewhere much closer, giving the impression that the cat was inside the apartment. D opened the front door and found it, small and gray, almost at his feet. The cat must have been right outside the door, aiming his wails at it. Without leaving off its cater-wauling, it raised its head and stood staring at D, half closing its eyes till they became two narrow yellow slits and then immediately opening them again. Instinctively, D, who a moment before had thought of going out to buy the newspapers as he did every Sunday, picked it up in his two hands, set it down again inside the apartment, went out the door and closed it behind him. In the hallway and on the stairs he could still hear its meows, insistently rolling on and on and on, as though they wanted something and weren't about to give up till they got it, and when he returned, with the newspapers under his arm, they had not changed. D opened the door and went inside the apartment. The cat was nowhere in sight and its meows sounded as if they were not coming from any one particular place but, rather, were occupying all the space in the apartment. D went on through the living room-dining room, onto which the front door opened, and through the other door, at the far end, leading to the bedroom, he could see his friend's body in the same position in which he had left her, drows-ing with her head buried in the pillow. The covers pushed down to the foot of the bed made her more stark-naked still. D entered the room, enveloped in the pitiful meowing, and saw the little gray cat, its eyes riveted on the naked body, standing on all fours in the middle of the other door to the room, as if it were unable to make up its mind to go in. The layout of the apartment permitted access to the bedroom from the entry hall by either of its two doors; one could go directly through the front room or go the long way round through the kitchen and the little breakfast room that opened directly onto it and onto the bedroom. D caught himself wondering whether the cat had taken this roundabout way or gone straight to the bedroom and was now merely pretending it couldn't make up its mind to go inside. Meanwhile, in the bed, beneath his gaze and the cat's, his friend changed position, stretching out her long leg and placing it right next to the other and putting one arm round the pillow without raising her head or allowing her chestnut hair to fall to one side and reveal her face. D went over to the cat, picked it up without its leaving off its meowing, left it in the hall again and closed the door. Then he sat down on the bed, slowly stroked his friend's back recognizing the feel of her skin against the palm of his hand, as though it alone could take him to the depths of the body stretched out before him, and leaned over to kiss her. She turned over with her eyes still closed, threw her arms around his neck raising her body so that it clung to D and with her mouth to his ear whispered to him to get undressed and continued to cling to his body as he obeyed. Later, as the two of them lay side by side, with their legs still entwined and enveloped in the mingled odor of their

11

bodies, she asked him, as though she had suddenly remembered something that came from much farther back, whether at some point or other he had let in the cat that had been meowing outside.

"Yes. When I went out to buy the paper," D answered, and realized that the meowing had stopped now.

"Where is it then? What did you do with it?" she said.

"Nothing. I put it out again. There was no reason for it to be here. I wanted it to surprise you while I wasn't here," D said and then added: "Why?"

"I don't know," she explained. "I had the impression all of a sudden that it was inside and it surprised me and pleased me at the same time, but I couldn't make myself wake up. . . ."

His friend stayed in bed till late in the morning, as D, sitting on the floor, alongside her, read the papers he had left on the table as he came in. Then they went out to have lunch together. The cat had not meowed again and it was not in the hall, or on the stairs, or in the lobby, and the two of them forgot the incident.

During the following week, though he did not hear it meowing again, D came across the cat several times, gray and small, looking at him for a moment, imperturbable on its mat in front of the apartment downstairs, curled up between the iron balusters on the stairs, going up or down in front of him without turning round to look at him, as though running away from him, or walking very slowly, right up next to the wall of the lobby, and when he closed the heavy glass door opening onto the street, leaving the cat behind, it seemed to him that it was acting more and more as though it owned the building and waiting mistrustfully for D to come back exactly the way the custodians did, feigning indifference there on its mat or curled up between the balusters on the stairway, with its frail and delicate look of a young cat that is never going to grow up and yet does not need anybody. Despite the fact that at times its silent presence was disquieting, there was always something tender and touching about it that made one want to protect it, giving one the feeling that its proud independence could not conceal its weakness. On one of these occasions, D came across it as he was going up to his apartment with his friend and she, noting the small gray figure, asked who it belonged to, but was not surprised when D was unable to answer her and immediately accepted as though it were the most natural thing in the world the supposition that perhaps it didn't belong to anyone, but had simply entered the building one day and stayed on in it. That night they were in the apartment till very late and as on many other occasions his friend, who always said she preferred it if D stayed in the apartment after being with her, did not want him to get up to take her home. The next time they saw each other, she remarked that when she left she had come upon the cat on the stairway and it had followed her down to the lobby, stopping only as she was about to step outside, as though it wanted to go out into the street and at the same time was afraid to, so that she had to be very careful as she shut the door.

"I felt like picking it up and taking it with me, but I remembered that you said it had chosen the building," his friend concluded, smiling.

D made fun of her love for animals and forgot the little gray figure again; but the following Sunday, on coming back after buying the papers he came upon the cat, which he had not seen as he went out, curled up between the balusters on the stairs. He went by it without its starting up the stairs in front of him and D, in surprise, turned round, picked it up, and went into the apartment with it. His friend was waiting in bed as usual and D, who had left her awake, tried not to make any noise as he closed the door, so as to surprise her. He was still holding the cat in his arms and it had curled up comfortably on his bosom with its eyes half closed. D could feel its little body, warm and frail, palpitating next to his. On entering the bedroom he saw that his friend had fallen asleep again, stretched out full-length on the bed, with her legs together and one arm over her eyes to shield herself from the light flooding in through the windows. There was no sign of expectation in her body. She was simply there, on the bed, beautiful and open, like a graceful, indifferent figure that held no secret for herself and yet at no time was unaware of the silent play of her limbs and the weight of her body, which gave form to its inherent reality, and was capable of causing her to be desired and of desiring herself in a double movement oblivious of its own starting point. D went over to her with the gray body curled up in a tight ball on his bosom and after looking at her for a moment with the same odd excitement as when he sometimes saw her fully clad in the company of other people, he very carefully set the cat down on her body, very close to her breasts, where the little gray figure appeared to be an object barely alive, fragile and terrified, unable even to move. On feeling the weight of the animal, his friend took her arm away from her

14

face and opened her eyes with a look of recognition, as though she had imagined that what had touched her was D's hand. Only on seeing him standing facing the bed did she lower her eyes and recognize the cat. It was lying motionless on her body, but on seeing it she gave a start in surprise, and the little gray figure rolled down alongside her on the bed, where it lay still again, unable to move. D laughed at her surprise and his friend laughed with him.

"Where did you find it?" she asked then, raising her head without moving her body to look at the little cat lying motionless at her side still.

"On the stairway," D said.

"Poor little thing!" she said.

She took the cat and set it down on her naked body again, close to her breasts, in the same place where D had put it before. He sat down on the bed and neither of them stirred as they watched the cat on her body. After a moment, the timid gray figure drew its paws out from under its body, stretching them out first on her skin and then setting off in an uncertain attempt to walk along her body only to come immediately to a dead stop again, as though unwilling to risk leaving it. Its yellow eyes turned into two narrow slits and then closed altogether. D and his friend again laughed in amusement, as though the cat's attitude were unexpected and surprising. Then she began to stroke its back with a gentle repeated motion and finally picked the little gray body up in her two hands and held it in front of her face, repeating over and over, "poor little thing, poor little thing, poor little thing," as she rocked it slightly from side to side. The cat opened its eyes for a moment and then immediately closed them again. With its paws hanging down, free of the hands holding it up by its body, it seemed much larger and had lost something of its frailness. Its hind paws began to strain downward, as though trying to support themselves on the body of D's friend and she stopped moving it from side to side and slowly lowered it, setting it down carefully on her breasts, where one of its extended paws directly touched a nipple. At her side, D saw how the nipple grew hard and erect, as when he touched her while making love. He stretched his arm out to touch her too and along with her breast his hand encountered the cat's body. His friend's eyes stared at him for the space of an instant, but both of them immediately looked away. Then she laid the animal aside and bounded out of bed in one leap.

For the rest of the morning they read the papers and listened to records, exchanging the same casual remarks as usual, but between the two of them there was a secret current, perceptible only from time to time and allowed to die down by tacit agreement, unlike that of all the Sundays before. The cat had stayed in the bed and when D's friend stretched out lazily on the sheets, without covering herself, as she did each Sunday so that the sun would touch her body along with the air that was coming in through the open window and D's gaze began to become one with that of the furniture, she stroked the little figure from time to time or placed it on her body to watch the way the cat, which appeared to have recovered the ability to move on its own, walked on top of her, placing its delicate feet on her belly or her breasts, or walked from one side of her to the other across her long legs stretched

16

out on the bed. When D and his friend went into the bathroom, the cat stayed on in the bed, asleep amid the rumpled covers that she had cast aside with her foot; but when they came out they found it standing stock-still in the living room, as though it had missed their presence and been looking for them.

"What are we going to do with it," his friend said, still wrapped in a bath towel, pushing her chestnut hair to one side and looking at the cat with mingled affection and doubt, as though they had realized all along that ever since the innocent joke at the beginning it had been with them the whole time.

"Nothing," D said in the same casual tone of voice. "Leave it in the hallway again."

And though the cat followed them as they went into the bedroom again to get dressed, when they came out D took the cat in his arms and unconcernedly left it on the stairs, where it stood, motionless, small and gray, watching them as they went down.

From that day on however, whenever they came across it, silent, small and gray, in the hallway with its yellowish half-light spotted with dark shadows, in the lobby or on the stairway, his friend took it in her arms and entered the apartment with it. She would put it down on the floor as she undressed and the cat would then stay in the room or wander indifferently about the living room, the breakfast room, or the kitchen, and then climb into bed and lie down on her body, as though from the first day it had become quite used to being there. D and his friend watched it, laughing, delighted at the way it made itself at home on her body. Every so often, she would caress it and it would close its eyes till they narrowed to a thin yellow slit, but most of the time she simply let it be there, hiding its head between her breasts or slowly stretching its paws out on her belly, as though it had not noticed her presence, until as she turned to embrace D it placed itself between the two of them and she pushed it aside with her hand. When D was waiting for his friend in the apartment, she always came in with the cat in her arms and one night when she announced that she hadn't found it in any of the usual places, the small gray figure suddenly appeared in the bedroom through the closet door. However, one day when she tried to feed it, the cat refused to eat a single mouthful, though she even tried taking it in her arms and bringing the dish up to its mouth. From the bed, D felt an obscure need to touch her as he watched her clasp the long slender figure to her and called to her to come to him. Now, on Sundays, the small gray figure had become indispensable next to her body and D's vigilant gaze noted its precise whereabouts, seeking at the same time to discover her reactions in its presence. She for her part had also accepted the cat as something that belonged to them both without belonging to anyone and compared her body's reactions to it with those which contact with D's hands produced in her. She never caressed it now, but instead waited to be caressed and when she lay drowsing with it at her side, on opening her eyes after falling asleep she also felt, as though it were something physical, covering her completely, the fixed gaze of the half-closed yellow eyes on her body and then she needed to feel D next to her again.

Shortly thereafter, D was obliged to stay in bed for a few days with an unexpected attack of fever, and she decided to arrange things so that she could stay in the apartment taking care of him. Dazed by the fever, plunged into a sort of constant half-sleep in which the dim consciousness of his aching body was at once unpleasant and pleasant, D noted almost instinctively his friend's movements in the apartment. He listened to her footsteps as she went in and out of the room and thought he saw her bending over him to see if he was asleep, heard her open and close one door and then another without being able to tell exactly where she was, perceived the murmur of water running in the kitchen or the bathroom and all those sounds formed a dense, continuous veil onto which day and night were projected without beginning or end, like a single mass of time within which only her presence was real, simultaneously near and far, and through that veil he seemed to note the extreme to which they were united and separated, as each one of her actions brought her into view before him, apart and secret, and for that very reason all the more his in this separation wherein she knew nothing of him, as though each of her acts were situated at the end of a taut, vibrating rope that he was holding onto from the other side, in the middle of which there was only a void impossible to fill. But when D finally opened his eyes all the way between two dream intervals without number, he could also see the cat following each of his friend's movements, without ever coming much closer to her, always a few steps behind, as though it were trying to pass unnoticed, but, at the same time, could not leave her alone. And so it was the cat, the presence of the cat, that filled the void that seemed to gape open inevitably between the two of them. In some way, it united them definitively. D went back to sleep again with a vague, remote feeling of expectation, which perhaps was simply part of the fever itself, but in the space of which there reappeared, again and again, distant and unreachable at times, immediate and perfectly drawn at others, invariable images of his friend's body. And then that very body, concrete and tangible, slipped into bed alonside him and D received it, feeling himself inside it, losing himself in it, beyond the fever, as at the same time he apprehended, through those very sensations, how she was always there before him, unreachable even in the most intimate closeness and therefore more desirable, and how she sought his body in the same way, until she left him alone in the bed again and began once more her obscure movements about the apartment, prolonging the union by means of the fragmented perception of them that fever gave to D.

During those long moments of concrete rapprochement, the cat disappeared from D's consciousness. On one occasion, however, he realized that it too was in bed with them. His hands had come upon the little gray figure as they wandered over his friend's body and she had immediately moved in such a way as to make the meeting more complete, but this end was never wholly realized and D forgot that there was an alien presence next to her. There had been no more than a brief ray of light in the middle of the dark lagoon of the fever. A few days later the fever broke as unexpectedly as it had come on. D began going out again and was with his friend in the company of others. There appeared to be no change in her. Her fully clothed body held the same secret that D suddenly wanted to bare before everyone; but as the moment approached when they would ordinarily have gone to the apartment she began, despite herself, without her apparently being consciously aware of it, to show clear signs of uneasiness and tried to hold off their arrival, as though there awaited her in the apartment a confirmation that she was unwilling to face.

When, after a number of delays inexplicable to D, they finally entered the building, the cat was not in the lobby, nor in the hallway, nor on the stairs, and as they made their way along them D noted that his friend was anxiously looking about for it. Then, in the apartment, D discovered a large reddish scratch on her back. They were in bed and when D pointed the scratch out to her she did her best to get a look at it, breathing hard, straining as though she were trying to feel it outside her own body. Then she asked D to keep rubbing the tip of his fingers over the scratch as she lay motionless, tense and expectant, until something seemed to break inside her and with panting breath she asked D to take her.

The cat did not appear on the following days either and neither D nor his friend spoke of it again. In reality, both of them thought they had forgotten it. As before the appearance of the fragile little gray figure between them, their relationship was more than sufficient for the two of them. On Sunday mornings, as always, she lay stretched out full-length on the bed, open and naked, displaying her indolent body as D whiled away the time carrying on the usual little everyday activities; but now she was unable to doze. Hidden behind her indolence and completely alien to her will, there appeared, more definite by the moment, an evident attitude of expectation which she tried to ignore, but which obliged her to keep changing position without finding repose. Finally, on returning after going out for the newspapers, D found her waiting for him with her body raised up off the bed, leaning on it with one elbow. Her gaze was frankly directed at D's hands, searching without even noticing the newspapers and on failing to find the hoped-for gray figure she let herself fall back on the bed, allowing her head to loll almost out of it and closing her eyes. D went to her and began to caress her.

"I need it. Where is it? We have to find it," she murmured without opening her eyes, accepting D's caresses and reacting to them with greater intensity than ever, as though they were one with her need and capable of provoking the appearance of the cat.

Then the two of them heard the long plaintive meows immediately outside the door in a transport of ecstatic happiness.

"Who knows," D said in a barely audible voice, almost to himself, as though all words were unnecessary, rising to his feet to open the door, "maybe it's simply a part of ourselves."

But she was unable to hear him, her body awaiting, tense and open, only the little gray presence.

The Square
PLACE

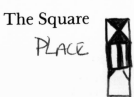

Every afternoon, on leaving his office, C headed for the square to which he had wanted to go nearly every day of his childhood with a definite goal in mind, reaching it only on a few unforgettable occasions. There in the antique ice-cream parlor under the arcades, to one side of the newspaper and magazine stands and the ever-changing stills from the films showing at the old movie house, he would meet a group of friends sitting in the familiar chairs with metal feet and backs and worn wooden seats around one of the little round marble-topped tables. Their number was not always the same, but invariably there was someone. At that hour, the permanent light that during the day shone down implacably on the laurel trees, the cupola of the bandstand in the center of the square, the whitewashed stones of the cathedral and the colonial buildings, with the incongruous rooster hailing the existence of the pharmacy on one of the corners, began to fade, becoming almost neutral before the sun hid itself from view and for an instant everything remained immobile and expectant, submerged in itself, as though the moment were going to last indefinitely and the late afternoon, refusing to surrender to the night, had extended the day beyond its possibilities. In the arcade the murmur of conversations, the characteristic sound of a dish on the marble and even the metallic scraping of a chair on the mosaic sidewalk were muted a little, taking on a deeper note and, all of a sudden, there was heard the excited song of innumerable invisible birds stirring among the shadowed branches of the laurels. Then the slow ringing of the cathedral bells rolled out over the plaza in ever-widening circles and it was as if the sound had induced the air to take on substance by marking itself out in its intangible space like the concentric motion of the waves that an object produces on falling into a calm lake. Meanwhile he ate the guanabana sherbet that the waiter had just left in front of him, idly participating in the vague general conversation. C was dimly aware of that barely perceptible conjunction of movements as something that habit has at last made part of ourselves. Thereupon, time started up again. Before dark, his friends began leaving for home and when night fell other customers occupied the table that they had abandoned with the memory of the ring of one last coin tossed on the marble table top, as chairs were pushed back. Night opened itself to a new day and in the afternoon, on leaving his office, C again headed for the square. And so the weeks and the months went by, one no different from the other in the sameness with which the hours repeated themselves. A wedding, a death, a friend who decided to leave the city, another baptism occasionally gave rise to an unexpected revelation of the passage of time, but, enclosed within a perfectly defined space, it did not seem to be taking on reality by moving forward, provoking, rather, backward looks that inevitably reached a dead end on the appearance of some old memory very soon dispatched to oblivion once more. In the late afternoon, beneath the arcades, the constant changes in the number of friends who gathered together round the little marble-topped table hid the definitive absences, but they were no less real for all that. Only the mysterious change in power of the light, the sudden song of the birds, and the long tolling of the bells remained invariable. That was how one day, carried along by the silent movement of the days which had finally left the table of the old ice-cream parlor almost permanently unoccupied, C too stopped going to the square. The last month, only he and one friend, sometimes two, had continued to meet under the arcades in the late afternoon. Soon the square lay definitely behind. Along with them, the city too left it by the wayside, obeying the involuntary movements that determined its growth. Though nominally it had not lost its symbolic character as a center, and the cathedral, the colonial arches of the palace of government, and the handsome facade of the house on which the escutcheon of the city had been engraved for the first time retained their prestige, to children the sherbets of the old-fashioned ice-cream parlor were no longer the ones most coveted, and among the laurels the bandstand on whose cupola the light settled without reflections as the bells began to ring out exposed to public view its rusty iron railings without its entering anyone's mind to protest, as the stains left by the swallows on the pavement gradually disappeared thanks only to the wind that erased them once the sun had dried them. Isolated in its own reality, the plaza was left without a memory. And to C, who along with the city turned his back on it, his so doing had no outward echo, although beyond his knowledge it had created a vacuum that no one seemed able to fill because it disclosed itself only in the form of sudden attacks of nostalgia for something the nature of which he was unable to express and which he quickly tried to erase, with a sort of shame in the face of the possibility that it would become noticeable and out of fear of the ability of this unknown something to paralyze him in a strange way, alienating him from the concrete realities that were immediately at hand and close to his heart. Nowadays, on leaving his office, he simply headed directly home. There, the mantle of the known enveloped him in its solid folds, though, at times, beneath him, the feeling of emptiness lay crouched, dark and threatening in its mysterious unreality and the trace of the days left behind disclosed itself then in all its profundity though nothing allowed him to recapture them, as meanwhile life or what once hid its emptiness appeared to pass by him without touching him, burning-hot and ice-cold, dense and indifferent, too vague to recognize, too intense to ignore, leaving him alone, helpless, with no one to turn to in order to find himself again, till one day, by chance, C found himself once again in the square in the late afternoon. There alongside him, the cathedral lay in massive repose in the sunlight. The light blurred its silhouette, making it reverberate along with that of the other buildings as though they had all been suddenly set in motion. A few undifferentiated figures were resting on the rickety benches of the square in the shadow of the laurels and as it filtered through the tops of them, that same light vibrating implacably on the buildings formed pools of shadow on the pavement that appeared to communicate with each other when the wind shook the branches of the trees. From the corner where he was about to get into his car, C saw the little marble-topped tables beneath the arcades enclosed within the straight lines of the metal chair backs and headed toward the old ice-cream parlor. As he sat down, his back recognized the trace of the metal chair back being etched upon it, as when he was a child. The waiter greeted him, recognizing him, just as when he had come to the ice-cream parlor of a Sunday morning with his wife and children; but now C saw him in a different way. His face, suddenly grown older, took him back to his immutable childhood desires and his never-recalled habits as a student, halting at a living and unalterable past instead of showing him the path of time. He ordered a sherbet and sat looking toward the square with the sensation of one who is about to enter a room in which everything will prove to be known to him even though he has never been in it. Then, just as when he used to meet with his group of friends and as on all the days that followed during his long absence, the afternoon began to give way before the night and that moment arrived in which for an instant all things hung suspended within themselves; but now C followed each one of the barely perceptible transformations with his spirit arrested at the highest point of an inexpressible elevation that rejected the motion of falling. The birds began to sing, invisible among the branches of the laurels, and then the bells sent forth their dull and prolonged sound above the bird song as though it had not come from the towers of the church but from much farther back, from a different space that washed over C like a vast wave, gentle, silent, and ever greater, extending without limits, as obscure and all-enveloping as a night made of light rather than shadows that had covered him with its quiet mantle. For the first time in a very long time, as he had not felt in the company of anyone or in the face of any event, C felt a silent and permanent happiness, and the square, to which he suddenly knew he would now definitively return every afternoon, was self-contained once again, enclosing everything in a time that is beyond time and for a fleeting but imperishable instant it restored to C all his substance.

Anticipation

FEELING

To Mariquiqui

A-1 and A-2 had known each other since childhood. They had never become friends. From the beginning a few differences, imperceptible to others yet, without their being aware of it, irreconcilable in their eyes, sustained a tenuous separation between the two of them, proving, by reason of their very subtlety, to be insurmountable. But obstacles of this type, which may not even come to be regarded as such, are in truth the ones that determine the form of relationships. Even though nothing appears to stand in the way of a rapprochement that one would suppose to be eminently natural, it never takes place. To pin down the precise reasons would prove to be a vain undertaking since these latter do not exist within the field of possible definitions. Nonetheless, the long acquaintance of A-1 and A-2 had favored their being brought together by chance on many occasions, to such a point that one could apparently state with certainty that their lives were following parallel courses. And, indeed, that was what was happening. Though not because they always remained close to each other, but because there existed no possibility of their ever touching each other, except in the improbable infinite that mathematics speaks of. Thus, A-1 and A-2, who had seen each other at a distance, being held by the hand or at least close beside their parents, at a time when, had they felt the impulse to speak to each other, they would not have been able to exchange more than a few words because of their limited vocabulary, saw each other again when they were left alone for the first time within the unknown precincts of school. Speaking at that point was more difficult still. Each took refuge in the incommunicable secrecy of his own emotions. An elderly schoolmistress, who resembled no one they knew, seated them on the same bench. They shared the games and activities aimed at keeping them occupied, but not their impressions of them. The same thing happened in grammar school, where they were not seated next to each other, though very often near each other. And in reality these first coincidences created a certain relationship between them, a very special, because indeterminate, communication, only it did not express itself in the usual ways. Its essential character was habit; during those years A-1 and A-2 were so accustomed to finding themselves inevitably in proximity that perhaps the sole way in which they could have become aware of it would have been for it to cease abruptly. But this was not what happened. When circumstances separated them many years had gone by and both of them had closer friends in whom the importance of closeness or distance was vested. But the separation signaled the beginning of an inversion which it was not possible to relate concretely to the fact of the separation itself, but which, in some way, perhaps made it evident, had there been anyone able to observe it from outside with an interest and a perspicacity that no one had any reason to possess. From a very early age, when his parents and a few of his closest relatives were his only company, A-1 presented an appearance that somehow informed against him. There crept into his face, into certain of his gestures and attitudes, a distant nostalgia for which there was no possible concrete justification, of which it could only be said that it went with his particular appearance as a given form of foliage goes with trees. A-2, on the other hand, had a number of siblings in addition to his parents. As might be expected they resembled each other and the most evident characteristic capable of defining them was strength. Nostalgia and strength are recognizable attributes. Throughout the long acquaintanceship of A-1 and A-2, beginning with the circumstances that favored their close proximity, these were perhaps the signs that separated them. A-1 was an excellent student all through grammar school, loved and sometimes spoiled by his teachers, something of a loner but with a secret admiration for certain of his schoolmates which he never managed to turn into a determination to approach them but instead kept his distance, perhaps because this admiration was aroused for the most part by the private recognition of a certain form of physical beauty. A-2, on the contrary, was never a good student. The teachers did not favor him with their affection, but he was always extremely popular among his schoolmates and his skill at competitive sports proved to be exceptional. On looking at him, it might often occur to one that A-2's strength was reminiscent of that of a wild beast one contemplates at a zoo. It accompanied him in a natural way and at times it surpassed him as though it were something that came to him from outside, in the same way as the vague nostalgia penned up inside A-1.

They thus spent, together and apart, their childhood years in the same provincial city, receiving the same religious education that attributed more importance to morality and sacred history than to secular subjects, in a school housed in an old mansion with any number of elegant rooms, with high ceilings and wood-framed French doors, fitted out as classrooms, surrounded by a wide porch with a beautiful balustrade, and possessed of vast cellars which it was forbidden to visit and which raised the level of the house in such a fashion that one arrived at its main entrance by way of a majestic staircase, with a great many enormous fruit trees all round, whose branches could be seen from most of the classrooms and whose tops were taller than the mansion. Besides being brought together in the school, where A-1 imagined daring adventures during class and A-2 waited impatiently for the bell signaling the end of it, the two of them ran into each other at many other habitual meeting places in the city, from churches to sports clubs, from movie theaters to the houses of certain of their schoolmates. But their differences remained irreducible. A great number of students found out, for example, that A-2, despite his justified reputation for bravery and determination, had not undergone an almost legendary test: climbing one of the fruit trees whose tall branches could be made to bend down over the roof terrace of the school if some sort of weight were forcibly brought to bear on them, but for that very reason scarcely able to withstand this weight, and then getting from these branches to the terrace, which could so easily be reached from so many other trees. On the other hand, A-1 carried off this feat all by himself one afternoon when everybody had already left school and nobody ever found out. He never forgot it. But how to communicate it? He had been so afraid that he would never be able to repeat it and nobody would have accepted a mere verbal report as true.

Then, A-1's now small family and he along with it, left that, to A-1, unforgettable provincial city and moved to the capital. The fruit trees there were different and their size ridiculous alongside those that A-1 remembered. The same thing happened with the number, form, and dimension of the rooms in the houses, with the furniture, with the streets, with the school run by fathers of the same religious order but without a single tree, not a building that had been made over into a school but one specifically planned and constructed to be a school, with a few dusty playing fields. But if A-1 did not forget his native city he did, on the other hand, lose almost all memory of A-2. He remembered some of his acquaintances occasionally, certain teachers less often still, and a few relatives only through the comments of his parents. It was not another life; it was another form of life; nonetheless, this change in form changed life. The vague nostalgia that always accompanied A-1 now had a concrete object; but, contradictorily, when it presented itself, A-1 rejected it, feeling ashamed. The foliage to which it owed its secret character had changed nature, even though A-1's appearance continued in some way to inform against him and his conduct with regard to possible friendships was very similar in the new school. On the other hand, for no logical reason, he ceased to be a good student. School had simply ceased to interest him in the same inexplicable way in which it had previously attracted him. He then began to have friends among the boys he met on the streets in the neighborhood where his new house was located. They were not friends, properly speaking; actually they were accomplices in the many violations of the rules of conduct that all of them committed. A-1 began to gaze from afar at a girl and then spoke to her and spent many mornings and many afternoons stretched out on the grass in front of her school. But he never managed to arrive at the point where his love had any importance for the one who was to him the absolute object of love. In this uncommendable fashion he made his way through high school. He was neither good nor bad; he was something much graver still and to his parents much more irritating and inexplicable: he was radically indifferent. If life could be a spectacle, to him that spectacle proved to be of little interest outside of the remote possibility, which he never managed to bring within his grasp, that his love would become accessible to the object of his love. And if life held a hidden promise in its future, there was no doubt that A-1 was not interested in unveiling it.

Meanwhile, in A-2 a similar transformation had taken place, though precisely the inverse. His strength was applied to his studies with the same dedication as previously to sports, and without abandoning these latter, he became an outstanding student. A-1 had disappeared from the pages of *Memoria*, the school's yearbook. A-2 still appeared on a great number of them. He had a steady girlfriend when he entered senior high school. She was the sister of one of his friends. They would sometimes leaf through back issues of *Memoria* together. In the earliest of them, the ones corresponding to grammar school, A-1 appeared. A-2's girlfriend remembered him and asked about him. A-2 had nothing to offer in answer. A-1 had simply left the city with his family and once he was gone his image too had lost all reality. The events of childhood that one remembers are related to oneself in a way in which A-1 was never related to A-2 during that period. But then A-2 also left the city, not with his family but because the time had come to enter university and both he and his parents agreed that it would be best for him to study for his degree in the capital. A-2 had often visited it in the past, but on finding himself in a student boarding house he felt the change in a way that might perhaps be related to the way A-1 had felt years before. It was logical that they should recognize each other when they met at the university. They were then closer than ever to becoming friends. They saw each other almost every day in class, surprised at having chosen the same field of study, and many events of the past came back to both of them without the difference that they had lived with back in those days coming between them. But the difference had not disappeared. The reversal that had come about, for each quite apart from the other, retained its effect. A-2 was a much more dedicated student than A-1 but during a fight, when A-1 was flung to the floor with his face covered with blood, it was A-2's strength that intervened to give him a helping hand. A small scar over A-1's left eyebrow remained forever after as a reminder of this episode, but for a long time he forgot all about it since, unlike A-2, he very soon lost all interest in the career he had chosen and before he reached his second year he left the university. This new separation again kept them from being anything more than acquaintances. A-2 frequently returned to his native city. A-1 never did. A-2 had another steady girlfriend there. A-1 kept making new friends and dropping old ones, he had no special girlfriend, and found a sedentary job in a bookstore. Then, with one of his perennial new friends, he went off on a trip, and his parents, who helped him out with a bit of money to enable him to take the trip, never found out how he had come by the rest. The owner of the bookstore, however, did find out. The quantity of books that were missing when A-1 left his job went beyond all possibility of his having made off with them without the owner's noticing. But even though his friend returned after a few months, A-1 was out of the country for more than a year and to the surprise of the owner of the bookstore, on his return he asked for his old job back. He did not seem to understand why the answer was no. He simply found himself another job, in a bookstore once again. He scarcely spoke of his trip, not even with his parents, even though he had spent several months in the north of Spain in the town where his father had been born, the latter having left it when still a child and never returned, just as A-1 had never returned to his native city. In his solitude however, A-1 appeared to have been converted to a new religion whose god was known to no one. For months he wrote endless letters to this new god. Then he ceased to do so. He had met an American girlfriend. They lived together for almost a year and finally she abandoned A-1 and went back to her country without his feeling any need to write to her.

Meanwhile, A-2 had finished his studies at the university. He returned to his native city to settle down and begin his career and a year later he married. He had had several siblings; he also had several children. He met with success in his profession, he was a well-off man, a happy husband, and an affectionate and responsible father. A-1, who had no profession and no money, also married however. But he was not a happy husband or an affectionate and responsible father. After three years, he obtained a divorce, when his only daughter was just one year old, and then, for no concrete reason after so long a time, he visited his native city. There is no explanation for this fact and the same could be said of what happened later. People are born, people grow up, people die. The years go by. The life of certain persons proceeds in a straight line; that of others appears to lack direction. A-2 occupied the first of these categories; A-1 the second. He married again, traveled with his new wife to Europe without visiting Spain, had two more children, was divorced again, his father died, his mother returned to the city where she and her son had been born. A-1, who had managed to become the owner of a small bookstore, visited her from time to

41

time and when he did so, quite consciously, he also visited his childhood. Sometimes he came to see his mother with one or another of his children, but, as with his mother, he was unable to speak with them of that childhood. As is natural, during these visits he met old schoolmates, among them A-2. They recognized him, said hello to each other, even embraced each other on a number of occasions, conversed together, and A-1 had the feeling that no one had said anything. Perhaps he alone had spoken on one occasion; he had spoken and written letters; but he had also lost the answers to these letters and this loss somehow seemed similar to the loss of his life. He was not unhappy. The problem was that he was not happy either. His oldest daughter had gotten married and two of A-2's children had done the same when, through one of those beautiful and strange coincidences whereby life brings together two points which are not related in any way, when both were just a few months away from becoming grandfathers, the two old acquaintances met in the main square of their native city, greeted each other with extraordinary joy, as though all of a sudden the fact that they had recognized each other meant something, crossed the square together beneath the dense laurels and as the cathedral bells announced the beginning of the end of the afternoon, decided to go have a coffee together at the old pastry shop and ice-cream parlor to which both had been going since they were children and with which the children of A-1 were unacquainted, just as the latter's mother never knew her father's town and the father had never gone back to it. Then A-1 told A-2 of his heroic exploit as a youngster when he had gotten from the tree to the roof terrace of the school. A-2, naturally, did not believe him nor was he in the least interested in this absurd recollection. Perhaps because both things irritated him, A-1 ordered another coffee without asking A-2 if he had time to go on with the conversation and unexpectedly he said:

"I'm certain that before dying everyone sees again the image that has been most important in his life and I think I know what that image will be for me."

No gesture, no look from A-2 gave proof of the least hint of curiosity on his part, but A-1 went on talking:

"Did you know that when I left the university I went to Europe and stayed for over a year? It was the most important experience of my life, or rather: it was the only experience in my life. I suppose I would be telling the truth if I were to maintain that it has been my one reason for living and for that reason I am unlike almost everyone else. My life has a meaning that cannot disappear even if the one to whom I owe it has been lost to me and remains present only as the force capable of conferring such meaning. You and I were both nineteen years old at the time. I expected and desired nothing and found everything; but since one cannot live with the whole because one does not recognize it, I lost it. Except that this loss is impossible. Something of it remains, a minuscule fragment that contains within itself that same totality and I am going to see that fragment before I die and recognize it. I made that journey with an acquaintance. It could have been you, but it was not. You were going on with the studies that I had abandoned. And very soon I separated from that acquaintance too, and continued the journey alone. Perhaps I didn't know what it consisted of back then, but what accompanied and guided me all the time was a very slight sensation of absolute irresponsibility. The sensation was very slight because this irresponsibility is so great that it would be intolerable if one were no longer able to recognize its true nature. More precisely: its true nature is a pure absence, the negation of any weight whatsoever, limitless freedom. Then all impressions, everything that our senses and our intelligence take in and preserve within us is incalculably vast and has no importance. I saw cities and monuments and public squares, very narrow streets and broad avenues, cathedrals and paintings, many paintings. I saw rivers and mountains, cypresses, dark hills and fields of wheat. I saw monasteries and olive trees, fig trees, groves of huge trees different from ours and as immutable and eternal as ours and I saw nothing because I was all that, as well as the books I sometimes read in languages I was barely able to understand. I was the bouts of drinking I gave myself over to and a continual mysterious withdrawal into myself that had to do with the certainty that I was nobody and would never again be anybody, merely the receptacle in which, with no continuity or any possible voluntary memory, all the sensations I received were accommodated. I saw the sea and it was always the sea, a sea like ours and a sea that was different though at times I felt it to be the same and at others unknown and surprising. I traveled along a narrow, unbelievably tortuous road on the roof of a ramshackle bus, amid mountains with enormous rock faces, greener and greener, and at one end of the road the sea also appeared at times. It was a very long journey. We stopped at many towns.

44

The road was in very bad condition, inconceivably badly laid out and the state of the bus was nothing great either. When we stopped in a town I drank wine and my companions on the roof of the bus warned me to watch myself on the curves. I climbed onto the bus very early in the morning and stayed on the roof of it almost the whole day. I saw, I felt, how the day was going by overhead, how places were becoming different, how the landscape was changing, how the sea suddenly reappeared. I was going to my father's town. I don't know why. He hadn't asked me to visit it and I had almost never heard it even mentioned. He had been born there, that's all, as we were born in this city; he had studied for a number of years with the fathers of some religious order, as we had in this city, and then he had left. But I remembered having heard him say that it was a town unlike any other, although once summer was gone it rained all the time and was freezing cold. This didn't mean anything. We all think of the place where we were children as somewhere different. But when I decided to visit my father's town it was summer. I was nobody and did not live in summer; summer, rather, lived in me. Nothing appeared to have an owner. Later on I seemed to have had much the same impression of the books in my bookstore. They are not mine; they have no owner, not only because nobody possesses a book, the object that every book is, but also because they are not the property of their authors either; authors, rather, belong to them. Immediately upon arriving in my father's town, after nightfall, I felt I belonged to it in that way. At some moment or other a very fine drizzle must have begun to fall because when I climbed down from the

45

roof of the bus my clothes and my skin were damp. The town was almost completely dark. There was no inn, no place to sleep. Only two cafés where a few old men and some youngsters were playing dominoes and without exception went on playing without turning round to look at me when I came in. I thought, I felt, that there was no object in my having gone there and I was a perfect idiot. But being a perfect idiot was perfect. Someone ageless passing by the houses of one town or another not knowing where he is going and as he walks along he allows his index finger to touch the walls of the houses. At the same time that I recognized myself as being a perfect idiot, the thought came to me as a possible solution to my problem that my father had a cousin who must still be living in the town. I remembered his name and surname, I remembered everything about him, though probably I had not heard him mentioned more than two or three times. I tried to imagine him and he looked like no one I could see in the cafés; he looked like no one I could imagine and therefore I was incapable of imagining him. Nonetheless, I made inquiries about him. I was asked in turn why I wanted to know his address. Because he was my uncle, I told them, and they gave it to me. He lived in a very large house with his five sisters, his wife, and his seven children, near the center of town, that is to say near the church, near the courthouse. But all that is of no importance. One always wanders about before getting to the place where one wants to be. One always reads useless books before finding the one that's needed. They gave me a marvelous welcome. They did not give me a marvelous welcome: they made me disappear. I was one of

46

them. I slept in the same bed as one of my cousins. I listened to his father as though he were my own speaking and discovered everything about his childhood that he had never told me. Speaking of this is all well and good, but it too is not important. I was part of the town. It is ten kilometers from the sea, joined to it by an estuary, known in those parts as a *ría*, and furthermore two rivers of different size, one of which passes directly behind the main square, loop round it at either end. The town is like a hole, hemmed in by water and mountains, motionless amid time, and yet it is rich and prosperous. My uncle was not rich. He had been so once but no longer was. This seemed to matter to no one. We simply lived in the town. To live in the town in summer was to go down the *ría* in a sailboat all the way to the sea, to fish and swim in the rivers, to get drunk on a dark wine in the dark cellar of the house of the father of one of my cousin's friends, to eat squid, mussels, and fried fish of all sorts in a tavern on the upper floor of a wooden house, to see from a mountain the panorama below, with the black slate roofs of the town, the trees in the square, the gardens, the rivers that surrounded it, the *ría* opening out, and in the distance, like a single blue line, the sea and alongside it the blurred silhouette of the other two towns located at each of the farthest points where the estuary ends. My uncle discovered that I worked in a bookstore. He had a library. He spoke to me of his readings, looked at me with astonishment, just as his sisters and his wife did, ran his bony hand through my hair and called me 'nephew.' It was my only identity since from that point on to the outside world I was simply his children's brother, the one who had one day arrived in the town and belonged to it. I went to the cafés. Not all that often because we didn't have time and like my cousins I didn't know how to play dominoes. But people knew me and recognized me as a part of El Campo, as they called my uncle's enormous house, topped by a tower with a pointed black slate roof from which one could hear the river flowing past, on the other side of which the main square of the town began. Then I met her. It was during the fiestas that for five days every summer were held in one of the towns at the seaside, with religious celebrations and worldly dances. My aunts attended church. My uncle stayed home. From the first day on I went with two of my cousins to the dances. We left after supper, crossed one of the rivers by way of the old bridge, took the road along the shore of the *ría* and walked the ten kilometers separating us from the neighboring town. She spent only the summers in the town. She lived in Madrid; but she had been born in a house beyond the river, one like my cousins'. She was part of the town, not like me, but from the beginning. I met her though because I too now belonged to the town. So many places, so many impressions and one alone encompasses them all and gives meaning to them. I hate succession, I hate time, I hate feeling that one has many lives and is not the owner even of the single one that justifies it. I have been telling you things that happened to me during a time in which time did not exist and I was always in the center of the day, a single day, just one, ever different and ever the same because its differences made me feel that nothing changed as I was simply the receptacle in which those differences became possible; but in order to tell you about them

I have used the memory of what I have gradually been recalling at the end of my entire life as though I had been familiar with all of them forever. This is not true. Many times those memories did not belong to me. For years I have totally forgotten them. Then, at certain moments, a few fragments of them have returned and I have again forgotten them because what appeared to be my life separated me from my life. I do not know how they have gradually been laid down and organized and built up, but I would hate myself if I wanted to convert them, if I tried to convert them, into a unity, for that unity exists only because its true meaning, the one in which all events, without being present, live completely, is contained in a single instant, in a single image, which may be incommunicable, but ought not to be incommunicable, which perhaps cannot be expressed only as such, but encompasses within its absolute power, within its unlimited dimension, within its nature forever outside of time although it happened within time, everything that need be expressed and the only thing that need be communicated. She too went to the dances and the gala celebrations held in those enormous pavilions open to the night that exist only in towns that do not use them more than once or twice a year for an entire week and then close them again. I cannot state precisely, knowing everything she means, everything her figure encloses, I have never been able to state exactly when I saw her for the first time, how she was dressed, whom she was with. One of my cousins, many of the boys in the town and in several of the neighboring towns were in love with her. What any girl at seventeen may always be: the image of love. I know that I danced with her, I don't know how I dared dance with her, I know that at one moment, that first night, I took one of the red carnations that were on the tables, gave it to her and she accepted it, though I don't know how I dared do that either. She smiled, tilting her head slightly to one side, not as virgins sometimes smile in medieval statues, but as those virgins smile in imitation of her. She laughed at my accent and at some of the words I used because they meant nothing to her and surprised her. But I'm telling you a story now. This is a succession of events which memory strips of their banality. When they exist in the present, their wonder and their authentic truth is that they have no importance. It is impossible to remember them. They do not exist, they have no consistency, no material substance; their one reality is the impossibility of remembering them without destroying what in truth they are: an instant, banal, absolute, a pure instant, with no other weight than their category as instant: like life. Because I did not know what was happening, because I did not know what I was doing, but was prisoner of a bedazzlement in which everything hides itself and falls silent, I stayed on in the town much longer than I had expected. On a night that ought to have been the last night for me, when the fiestas were ended, I went over to her as she was walking down the main street with other girls and told her I didn't want to leave. She answered that she didn't want me to leave either and that I should stay. That is what she must have said. It is impossible for me to preserve the memory of such definitive words. For months I had been no one. The absolute fullness of being no one is probably contained in that moment because I must then have been everything. I can be precise and tell you, without the least risk of being mistaken, that some time later, that an eternity later, but still during that same night that might have been the last and was an indifferent night alien to time, alone at her side, walking at her side, with the promise to see each other the next day that we must have made each other at some moment, I accompanied her back across the river by way of the old bridge, till we were close to her house, and there, at some point beyond the bridge, she stopped, bent her head slightly downward and I did what her gesture bade me do: I kissed her on the forehead. On the way back there was almost no one walking along the main street or else I was unable to see anyone. I cannot tell you what I felt, not because I do not remember it, since even though I have not thought of it for years I must not have ever forgotten it; if I cannot tell you what I felt it is because I felt nothing, I did not feel myself, I saw nothing, I heard nothing, I did not realize that I was walking: empty fullness. And so, in order that that absolute might have some reality, once I arrived at my uncle's and found him in his library I told him everything. He listened to me, gravely and intently, and then told me I should go to bed and not forget anything. I obeyed. The cousin who slept with me was already in bed. He was the one who was also in love with her. I told him everything. When I fell silent at last, he asked me in a very low voice not to say any more and come to bed. I was the one who turned out the light. I think we both lay awake listening to the other not sleeping, but the following day he was my same cousin as ever, the one whom I had met less than three weeks before and who was much more than my

cousin. I was the one who was not the same. I abandoned my openness to everything and everyone; I
ceased to be wholly present in places, theirs entirely.
I was hers alone, I existed only in her, I lived only to
feel her live. I have married twice, fathered three
children; much time has gone by. I have often lived for
years on end as though I had forgotten all that. I spent
several months with her, about which I could tell you
nothing because I have forgotten most of the concrete
events, but not their splendor, and what is more, I now
know what that splendor was capable of awakening.
We were together in the town for several weeks. Then
she went off to Madrid and I followed her. We were
together there for more than two months and then my
visa expired and my money ran out and I had to leave,
certain that I would come back very soon. I never did.
I never saw her again. And I find myself unable to recapture the image of our farewell in the railway sta-
tion. I know only of my devastating need in the
beginning to see her, of my inability to believe that it
was not possible, of the absolute presence of her
absence that made me nothing more than a pure
nostalgia. I wrote to her for months. Many letters,
countless letters, very long letters. She wrote to me too.
Then suddenly, I don't know why, I still don't know
why, I imagine because that succession I hate, because
that time I hate, because this life in which we are
immersed devours everything and kills everything, it
seemed that it was meaningless to live in order to write
letters and I stopped. I took a mistress. Maybe that
might explain it. At any rate it's a beautiful, idiotic
explanation. I might say: I fell in love with another
woman. One does not have just one love and there is

such a thing as the reality of presence and desire. How stupid! All that is false because it is true only insofar as it is the condition of imbeciles. The truth is that many are called and few. . . . I stopped writing to her. I lost her letters. I don't even have her letters, only those bits and pieces of memories that have kept appearing down through the years. The main square of the town, where we would sit for hours at a time on one of the benches. There were eucalyptus trees and poplars with leaves whose undersides were silvery and I don't know what other trees. Nor do I know if it is true that we sometimes would hear the church bells. From one end of the square, with our backs to the main street of the town and the row of houses that in that particular spot lined only one side of the square, we would lean on the balustrade and watch the river flowing past, on the other side of which was my house, my uncle's house. I would kiss her on the hair, on the forehead, on the cheeks, and on the mouth. We would then leave the town and walk along the highway that led away from it in two directions on either side of the *ría*. A few times we strayed amid the pines and laurel on a mountainside. In Madrid I remember waiting one morning, the first morning, leaning against the trunk of a scrawny chestnut tree, for her to come out of her building, the building she lived in, near El Retiro, in the Calle de Alcalá. That was who I am. What does that have to do with the one I am now? We saw each other every morning, every afternoon till it came time for her to go back home for the night. We also walked beneath the trees in El Retiro and sat on the benches. It was autumn then. Nature changes and the light is different and the trees contain every color in their leaves and begin to lose them and it is a beautiful sight to see them on the ground; but this becomes visible only now because I remember it as experienced from the point of view of love and at the time love, which cloaks everything, permitted me to see nothing of that except as one of the forms of its representation. We also visited the Prado Museum sometimes. Before a Titian, I felt her body very close to mine. We even went to the movies, as though wasting time didn't matter, as though no time was misspent. But if I can tell you all this that is vague and fragmentary and fails to explain what she was and what I was because I lived through her, it at least shows that if my life matters or means something I am certain that it is only because it is useless, senseless, full of illusions and tricks of the imagination and means nothing above and beyond my precise ability to enable that unique image of her and what I owe her to be present in me. When no more than ten days had gone by after what should have been my last night in the town and about which I have forgotten all the details though not the total truth of what existed, she was obliged to go with her family to a hotel at a spa near the town and was gone for several days. I went back to the rivers once again with my cousins and again swam in those rivers and in the *ría*, I went back to the upstairs tavern once again and to the cellar of the father of one of their friends where we drank dark red wine directly from the casks and above all I talked with my uncle. I don't know what I gave voice to; I know that he listened to me with what is also love and told me that she was not in good health though that could matter only to those who were seeking certainties and I was not one of their number. Then the miracle came to pass, the one that it is impossible for me to say at precisely what moment in the sum total of the passing years it revealed itself to me as miracle. I did not know exactly when she was going to return. She had told me that she would be gone for five to fifteen days. The bus she would be arriving on came through the town around noon and stopped for a moment opposite the main square, alongside one of the cafés which had a little outdoor terrace. From the fourth day on, after 11:30 I sat down to wait on one of the benches in the square or in that café and saw the bus come in and stop, and she did not get off and I don't know what I felt, but it was as though everything had become empty and there existed only the need to see her, for her not to be far away, as far away and as present as she was during what was to be my last night in the town and I had seen her walking down the street with her girlfriends and the helplessness, the fear in the face of a future in which she had disappeared for me and I would not see her again were so great that I decided to go to her and speak to her. I went off to look for my cousins so as to kill the rest of the day, as though I were still the same as they. Some five days must have gone by in this way. I cannot be certain whether everything I have told you can serve to justify the importance of what happened then or lend it credibility, and if I try to recount what happened I feel that words dissolve it, that they turn it into a mere event, into something too concrete. And it isn't. It's nothing. It's everything. It lacks meaning and includes all the senses. It is the total image I have of the perfection of life, of its supreme beauty, when it is life alone and at the same time something more than life because it includes it, contains it and represents it, maintaining itself within it, and simultaneously standing outside it, like an image that is possible only because the world exists yet at the same time does not belong to the world, does not belong to anyone except itself because as an image it knows nothing of such belonging. Is that understandable? It cannot be understood. It simply is and negates all meaning, but it contains all meanings because, even unknowingly, one has learned to recognize all meanings through it. It frightens me to tell you this. It is something that should not be spoken of and I cannot keep from telling you so as to know once again that it is true, just as I felt it on a day I do not remember, one on which I suddenly understood everything I had had and why my life mattered. More than thirty years have gone by since that moment, thirty years which, with the nineteen before, the age I was when I met her and began to live what I have tried to tell you, comprise my entire life. Nonetheless, I believe that I am able, that I must be able, despite all my fears, to reconstruct it down to the last detail, with the absolute precision which it will have when I see it again before I die. All the foregoing, what you have been hearing me say, is no more than the indispensable frame for enclosing that image and it is the image alone that makes the frame possible and necessary. I was in the café. The bus pulled in. I rose to my feet and walked a few steps toward it and then she got off. The moment in which she stood there in the street forms that absolute image which I recaptured and which in its simplicity and in its supreme absence of importance, its negation of all transcendence but also of all immanent temporality encompasses all possibilities and all meanings. Round her neck she was wearing a blue silk foulard that my father had given me before I left on my travels and that I had given in turn to her. She was dressed in a long-sleeved blue cotton shirt-waist and a skirt of the same color and material. She had on low-heeled suede shoes, blue as well. That blue. How to explain it to you? It is simple and unique. No comparison with any natural object or with any work of art would be of help. It was the blue that she was dressed in. That will have to do. In the total presence of that image she and blue are the same thing. They are the symbol of something that symbolizes nothing, that merely makes itself present to itself. She was standing there, slim and young and fragile and mysterious and immediate. She was innocence, untouched, forever untouchable and forever present to grant us through its pure existence the possibility of knowing. Her purity enveloped her, created a halo round about her, and that halo was invisible and existed only within her. Its materiality asserted itself by vanishing. The world did not surround her. It was surpassingly beautiful and splendid and eternal because it did not exist but, rather, lost itself in her. All of this that I have told you holds only an instant; it contains no succession. As I saw it, as I see it again now, as I shall see it before dying, there was no before nor was there to be an after. I was unable to think it, but I knew that because everything was enclosed in her young figure clothed in blue, everything was going to remain still, motionless forever. And that stillness, that immobility are perfection. I can go on speaking to you still. I can tell you of the oval of her face, of her hair neither long nor short, of the convex curve of her forehead, of her full mouth, of the indescribable color of her skin that is nonetheless a color, of her left leg thrust just slightly forward from the moment she alighted alongside the bus. It was not possible and therefore it was possible that in something so simple, so common, so ordinary so many things should be encompassed and I should fail to notice because her presence alone blurred all these things, made them simple and common also, turned them into what they truly are: everything and nothing, something inexhaustible, without end, whose form of existence is a pure nonexistence and yet it cannot be doubted that they exist because her presence makes them manifest. She saw me and gave the faintest of smiles, as she always did, tilting her head slightly to one side. I must then have come over to her, I must have spoken to her, I must have entered time, and fleetingly, as always happens within it, I was happy. But meanwhile, without my knowing it, the image had fixed itself which I would recapture later and of which I have just spoken to you."

A-2 put out one last cigarette in the ashtray that one of the waiters must have emptied several times. Perhaps he was a bit surprised and disconcerted; perhaps he had not listened intently to the whole story; perhaps he had been bored for a few moments and it was also possible that he had felt impatient and irritated at what might have appeared to him to be an abuse of the fact that they were old acquaintances. In any case, he scarcely looked at him, avoiding his eye after putting out his cigarette, as if he did not know, and this ignorance gave rise in him to a certain fear, exactly what sort of face he would encounter on gazing directly at it. Meanwhile darkness had fallen and at that hour many people were coming out of the movie theater near the café. A-2 felt that, in any event, he had to break the almost palpable silence that had fallen between him and A-1. He tried to attribute less importance to his anxiety, to speak as if he had felt nothing special, as if nothing in A-1's story had troubled him in any way, as if he were merely tired, and also, though he had done his best to appear to be trying to hide it, bored.

"I don't know why you've told me that whole long story," he commented.

"I don't know either," A-1 replied. "I suppose it was to make that image I recaptured appear once more and project it before it enters the place where it will find forever the fullness of being that rightfully belongs to it."

The Seagull

To my children, Mercedes and Juan

They had been walking along the seashore almost since the beginning of the morning, on the narrow strip of firm sand, wet by the gentle going and coming of the little waves that erased their naked footprints as they silently spread out across the burning-hot beach, as though they had become accomplices of the, for them, unwitting intention not to turn back, and from the beginning too, the seagull followed them, flying just a short distance behind their backs, never once getting ahead of them, until it was now the one living presence that could bear witness to their double solitary figure, united in its separation and alike in its difference. Around it, around the barely adolescent double figure, the boy in heavy white cotton pants with the legs rolled up to uneven lengths and his shirt, also white, tied round his waist once the sun's piercing rays began to hit his back, with the shotgun hanging suspended from his left shoulder and his

63

hand every so often touching the shiny butt, and the girl with her tight-fitting pale blue shorts leaving her long golden-brown legs free and her thin sleeveless blouse revealing the no less lovely contours of her arms, there was no space, only, above the delicate murmur of the sea, light, a single, intangible light, beneath which colors and shapes vanished.

The sea was simply the mirror on which, at the crest of a gentle wave, the luminous emptiness of the sky suddenly glinted, its tenuous movement disappearing with no transition in the burning brightness of the sand bounded on the opposite edge by the fringe of bushes, also colorless, which appeared to belong neither to the water nor to the land and behind which there stretched only the limitless space of the sky.

They had begun their walk by heading away from the houses bordering the shore, not knowing why, merely to be moving about, to confirm the solitude in which they had once again found themselves, and now the whole world seemed to be far away; but they were not alone; in the clear radiant light, the flight of the seagull made the weightless texture of the air tangible, as though its dazzling whiteness negated the other reality of white; present even though neither of the two had at any moment turned round to look at it and the seagull had never flown ahead of them, as though it were only escorting their ignorance of the reason for their movements.

Summer was already ended. An end that brought with it the beginning of nothing; but, as on the second day, she had appeared, very early in the morning, from among the vacant houses, and come over to sit down beside him as he gazed at the colorless sea with his legs drawn up, his arms circling his knees, and the shot-gun over his shoulder. Later on they started walking. When he stood up, he had taken her hand to help her to her feet and for the first few steps he continued to hold it in his: the thin hand that, on the first day, had felt fragile, as though he might break it, make it disappear by the application of no more than a slight pressure, on taking it to say goodbye to her, darkness having already fallen, after they had roamed along the seashore and among the lonely houses.

"Look at the stars!" she had said then in her perfect Spanish, though with an accent different from his, the dissimilarity making them laugh at first, and on lifting his head, following the movement of her endlessly long neck, it seemed to him that before that moment he had never seen the sky or the night. Then and thereafter, he was nonetheless full of memories prior to her, solitary memories, which her appearance and the tension that followed, after three dazzling days, during the long months of summer, had con-signed to oblivion.

During those months he often felt, though with fury now, that everything was the same as the first after-noon by the sea on the porch of his parents' house, which, to add insult to injury, was now also hers. All he could think of then was her name, as though it belonged to no one and at the same time was every-thing. Katina. When she told him her name, after he thought he had heard it without understanding what it was her father had said, the three syllables stood forever after for that figure as slender as his own and no less tall than he, enclosing her skin already lightly tanned, her blue eyes shielded by unbelievably delicate, nearly transparent eyelids, edged with long eyelashes as black as her hair, parted in the middle and falling to either side of her shoulders, and as the double arch of her eyebrows, around which her entire face was arrayed, with its broad forehead, its straight nose, its prominent cheekbones that made the cheeks look slightly hollow, its pale thin lips and the firm jawline, ending in the round chin that gave the long curved neck the appearance of being completely independent. Everything about her was exotic and different, but he knew that she too doubtless saw him in the same light. On the other hand, when he told her what his name was, it meant nothing and made him feel ashamed. Luis. A single syllable, and trailing after it perhaps only an inexplicable fury. Up until then they had been like two restless wolf cubs eying each other warily even though they belong to the same pack, their muscles tense, barely containing the impulse to spring, sitting on the mosaic floor, each alongside his and her mother and father, who were speaking together in English, a language which, without their yet being able to tell each other so, neither of the two of them knew; and they were such handsome youngsters that finally even their parents could not help noticing their expectant attitude. His parents had come to the summer house before anyone else, as planned, there to await hers: the German friends whom they had met on their honeymoon, who had been living in the capital for two years and had now accepted their eager invitation to spend the summer with them. It turned out later that even though her parents hadn't so much as touched Spanish in those two years, Katina had mastered it perfectly after three months at a school where everybody nonetheless spoke to her in German.

"Your name means Ludwig," she said to him, laughing, when she learned what it was.

That made two syllables, but by nightfall she had already gone back to the one inevitable original syllable, changing it first to Lud and then, definitively, forever, to Dwig, a word he couldn't even pronounce, which according to Katina was not German or anything at all and so, from the beginning, it belonged to her alone. It had not been easy, however, to get on closer terms. Luis's father spoke to her in English first; instead of answering him Katina spoke in turn to her father in German; the two fathers again spoke together in English; then her mother spoke to her in German and finally, Katina spoke to Luis in Spanish. He was as terrified as though they had suddenly flung him into an abyss and the parents of both of them laughed, but when, following his mother's suggestion, he finally found himself alone on the sandy shore with Katina, who laughed as she spoke of the grownups' idiotic question—"Is that the right way to say it?"—making him laugh too, it was Katina who immediately explained that Katina was a nickname but she would never, never tell him her real name.

"It's not something awful; but I don't like it," she explained, turning her head toward the house for an instant and then riveting her eyes on him.

Luis had overcome his initial fear, but now he was disconcerted.

"I don't have many girlfriends," he said. "Here . . . ."

"I know," she interrupted him and fell silent, waiting.

He smiled, suddenly charmed.

"Maybe that's a good thing, right?" he said then.

Before them was the sea and round about them everything was known. The parents of the two of them sitting on the porch seemed very far away. Katina's eyes followed his.

"I love them lots," she said as if to make amends for having made fun of them. "Do you love yours, too?"

"Yes," he said unashamedly.

"Okay then," Katina said, that basic question having been settled. "What shall we do now?"

From that moment on, for the next three days, Luis tried to act as their guide. The sea was a little roiled still and the waves stained with algae broke heavily on the sand on which the same algae lay drying. First they walked along the beach, heading nowhere in particular. She looking toward the sea; he toward the houses, overcoming the temptation to tell her who would be coming to live in them in a few days, aware that for Katina mere names could mean nothing. The strong sea breeze blowing wrapped her thin cotton dress tightly about her legs and when, without a word of warning, she suddenly sat down on the sand to take off her shoes, her skirt slid up over her thighs, baring them completely. Standing alongside her, he had to make himself look away toward the long pier extending far into the water, farther on, at the harbor.

"Look, a German boat may have just come in," he said when he looked her way again.

"So what?" Katina answered with a shrug. "I'm not homesick." She rose to her feet and holding her skirt up with her hands walked farther and farther out into the water almost to where the waves were breaking. The breeze ruffled her black hair, tossing it over her face.

"It's warm," she said almost in surprise, turning to Luis, still sitting next to her sandals as though he felt it his duty to guard them.

"I know," he answered, in a condescending, perhaps slightly scornful tone of voice.

"Aren't you coming in?" she persisted.

"No, I'll wait for you here," he said and the thought occurred to him that once she came out he would take her inland, to the coconut groves, beyond the houses, where his skill at climbing the smooth-ringed trunks might surprise her.

During dinner, in fact, Katina gave her parents an enthusiastic account of how Luis had climbed the palms and he knew all of a sudden that that was what she was doing because she kept turning around to look at him, although he could barely make his name out amid the music of the long and short vowels that seemed to form just one word; but after that it was the grownups who talked and the two of them, each sitting on one side of the table, simply looked into each other's eyes with the merest hint of a smile between one mouthful and another.

When they'd finished everyone went out onto the porch again, where there was a strong, almost fierce wind blowing and as their parents swayed to and fro in their rocking chairs speaking between brief silences, Luis and Katina sat on the steps leading directly down to the sand, very close to each other, looking toward the sea which, lost in the darkness, was a mere continuous murmur.

"What part of Germany are you from?" Luis had asked her then, though his parents had told him before, and she answered:

"From München," pronouncing the word in such a way that it sounded different to Luis and turned the city into another place from the one he had imagined.

Then it was he who spoke, of his cousins and friends and of visits to his grandparents' old hacienda, till all of a sudden Katina stretched and gave a gaping yawn that ended in a deep sigh.

"Katina's tired," Luis's mother said, leading him to think fearfully that they had been listening to them the whole time and therefore overhearing some of his exaggerations, bordering on outright lies; but his mother merely said something to Katina's mother in English and then told him to show her to her room and go to bed too if he wanted to.

Katina kissed her parents and Luis's as she said goodnight and he felt obliged to do the same, ending with his father, who proudly gave him what was almost a hard cuff on the cheek.

They went up the stairs together and Luis hesitated at the door of the bedroom that Katina had been given, which before then had always been his grandmother's room. Katina yawned again and her blue eyes filled with tears, gleaming more brightly still.

"Well then. . ." Luis said.

"No, come on in," she said, opening the door.

Her suitcase lay on the bed. Katina went straight to it and began to fling things out of it, leaving them strewn all about, as Luis stood waiting near the door still, admiring her. Then she suddenly stopped and looked toward the window.

"You can hear the sea," she said in genuine surprise.

"Of course," Luis answered proudly. He opened the window and the murmur entering the room was more distinct.

"How marvelous, Dwig!" she said, her deep blue eyes opened wide in surprise and happiness. "I like everything, everything pleases me!"

It seemed to him that her remark sounded like something a grownup would say and he was embarrassed, but she was now walking over to the window and leaping lightly out onto the terrace from between the two open casements. He followed her and it was then that Katina told him to look at the stars and after remaining silent for a moment she held out her slender, ever so slender hand, said goodnight to him, and went back into her room through the window. Instinctively, Luis went to his room too and once in bed, in the dark now, only the present began to exist for him, with no anticipation of the future or a much more impossible look backward, to where there was as yet no Katina.

On one of the afternoons, the second of their first three days alone, as the parents of both were taking their afternoon nap, Luis broke into one of his uncle's houses through the back door, having remembered seeing a large atlas there, and lying on the upper terrace on the mosaic tiles cast in shadow by the walls, he and Katina went through it, thanks to his more or less stubborn insistence, to see how far it was from her city to his; but Katina was not interested in maps or confirming facts. She was at least as good a swimmer as he and her endurance matched his, but Luis was better at water-skiing and the first time she had a bad run she stopped trying. The first morning, on coming downstairs, half asleep still, in shorts and without a shirt, to have breakfast, he found her already at the table in a bathing suit and when, once breakfast was over, she stood up, her slender body, barely covered by the little red bikini, was so beautiful that he didn't even notice how intently he was contemplating her, all notion of the need to finish his chocolate milk gone, thinking only about going back upstairs to put his bathing suit on and go out onto the beach with her.

She waited for him on the porch, in one of the rocking chairs, without rocking, her long legs with still slightly nubby knees stretched straight out in front of her and one foot on top of the other, nibbling a cracker with jam and with the red straps of her bikini top untied, hanging down over her mirror-smooth belly, and the moment he appeared on the porch she set the cracker down on the arm of the rocker, not noticing that the abrupt movement with which she rose to her feet made it fall to the floor, and ran down the beach to the water, tying the straps round her neck as she went, enveloped in the steady morning light, without contrasts, as though her figure had been born of the light or were part of the sea, moving in an emptiness that received her without the least resistance. He followed her instinctively, running too, and they reached the water's edge at almost the same time, whereupon she dived in, followed also by Luis, almost without a moment's hesitation, disappearing under the water, a bit roiled still, a few yards farther out from the place where the breaking waves had made her raise her arms for an instant to keep from getting splashed. As he lost sight of her under the water, Luis began to swim without putting his head under, slowly drawing away from the shore and a few moments later he saw the black head reappear not very far away and Katina continued to swim farther out. He caught up with her and swam at her side till she stopped where neither of the two could touch bottom any longer. She pushed her hair back from her face, opened her blue eyes with drops of water shining in the lashes, and smiled at him as though certain that she would find him at her side.

"It's so odd that the water's warm," she said, slightly out of breath, as her slender hand repeated the gesture of pushing her hair back. "I could stay here all the time."

Luis looked at her, gasping a bit for breath too, noticing how the sea made her body rise and fall with the same gentle rhythm as his own.

"Your hair . . ." he said.

"What about it?" she asked.

"I don't know. . . . It's like . . . like a picture frame."

Katina looked straight at him with a mischievous gleam in her eye.

"I'm going to cut it someday," she said then in a very serious voice, repeating the gesture of tossing it back and then smiling.

Never, Luis thought, never, as when she remarked that she would never tell him her name; but she said nothing more, and the two of them simply lay alongside one another, rocked freely by the sea, united and separated by it, till without warning Katina, as though suddenly self-absorbed, began swimming parallel to the shoreline and he hesitated for a moment before making up his mind to follow her.

They did not get out of the water till the parents of both appeared on the shore, planting an enormous green and blue beach umbrella in the sand, and Katina lay down placing her head on her father's belly as he was sunning himself with his eyes closed outside the sheltering shadow of the umbrella and he gave a start on feeling her wet hair touch him. Luis's father laughed as he stood at a prudent distance and Katina then said something to her father, which Luis was of course unable to understand, showing him her hands all wrinkled from being in the water for so long.

Luis's mother warned Katina, speaking very slowly, as though she would have a hard time understanding her, to beware of the sun and Luis, smiling to himself at his mother's unnecessary caution as she spoke, had the sudden thought that the sun would never do anything to her, not realizing that to him this was not possible because Katina was part of the light, was light itself, with no limit, incarnated in her person beyond all space, apart from all contingency; but when his father suggested taking the guests for a boat ride along the coast and asked him to go with him to get the motorboat which with the help of the village fishermen they had launched the morning before and was now rising and falling to the beat of the waves offshore, Katina and her parents and his mother all donned blouses to protect themselves and Katina and her mother straw hats with pointed crowns and the broad brims pulled down, Katina's with a blue ribbon, which she carefully tied underneath her chin, shading herself with her arm as well and looking at the white shoreline standing out in the distance, so that, seated at the very end of the prow, each time he turned to look at her, as the spray raised by the motorboat spattered his body, the upper half of her face lay in shadow and he was unable to tell whether or not she was looking at him too.

They then swam for a good while around the boat, far from shore, in the deep green waters, and Katina appeared to be concerned only with her father and with attracting the attention of Luis's father; but at a moment when he was resting with his arms leaning on the edge of the boat and his head on top of them, he felt someone pulling on his legs under the water and a second later Katina's head appeared, shaking her hair from her face and smiling at him from the opposite edge and then, the next day, when they had a try at water-skiing, her attention was entirely concentrated on him. Around that time, the previous afternoon, as the grownups were taking their siesta, they had walked to the harbor along the highway that the back of the whole long row of summer houses overlooked. Katina, who had left the house barefoot despite his warning, had gone back for a pair of sandals the minute her feet touched the hot pavement of the highway, but all she was wearing besides were white shorts and a yellow bra top as skimpy as the one to her bikini and, spellbound, he didn't even think to tell her that nobody went to the harbor dressed like that, feeling deep down that she was untouchable and had every right to do exactly as she pleased.

First they went to the end of the long pier, where there was no German vessel in, but two Norwegian ones, a Turkish one, and a little Mexican coastguard boat. Katina called out something in German to the officer, impeccably dressed in white, aboard one of the Norwegian ships, who was looking at them from the pilothouse and, taken by surprise, he answered immediately, all enthused, and came down for them straightway and took them aboard the ship, where he went on talking with Katina, smiling continually, as he showed them the various appointments, in response, Luis thought, to questions from Katina, who went on talking with the officer while at the same time she kept continually turning round to smile at Luis and at one moment when their guide had his back turned to them she gave a scornful shrug and stuck her tongue out at him. Then, once the two of them were back on the pier, as she waved goodbye to the smiling officer, she remarked to Luis:

"He's a fool and thinks we're fools too. Poor thing."

Luis felt rewarded for having had to keep silent for such a long time and, sure of himself again, walked alongside her, aware that the officer was looking at them from the loneliness of his ship, to the opposite side of the pier, where Katina began talking again, but in Spanish this time, with one of the seamen, drenched in sweat and his swarthy-skinned torso bare, sitting on a plank suspended above the water painting the hull of the Mexican ship. The seaman's explanations of how the little gun located on the prow operated were rather confusing and Katina immediately ended the attempt to converse.

As they walked back along the pier in the blinding light of the afternoon sun, the white line of summer houses looked at one and the same time close at hand and far away, as though they were in another space impossible to reach from the pier, and Luis suddenly felt that, unlike him, Katina was not part of the world that they encompassed, though neither did she belong anywhere else; she was simply there, walking next to him, with her hair ruffled by the wind, pushing it back now and again from her face, and perhaps at some moment, precisely because her presence was so absolute that he was unable to think of anything but the nearness of her, without even being conscious of its importance, but simply enjoying it as a part of himself, foreign to him, even though, in some way, he had always had it, it had always accompanied him, without, of course, his ever becoming aware of it except in the instant in which, without in the least expecting it, it had become real, it might disappear in the same way. That all-powerful and intangible reality gave a new and different character to the little commercial area of the harbor, in which there were any number of shadowy shops of all sorts that gave off countless different smells and among whose miscellaneous objects Katina poked about endlessly, inspecting them all until, as Luis had planned, they sat down at one of the marble-topped tables of the ice-cream parlor to have a cold drink; but she took only a few sips of hers and immediately got up to have a look at the series of postcards on display near the entrance, showing different spots along the beach and the port taken from such odd angles and tinted in such surprising colors that they were unrecognizable.

"Who are you going to send all those to?" Luis asked with a vague fear, equally unrecognizable to him, when she returned to her place with an enormous number of postcards.

"Not to anybody," Katina answered. "They're for me."

She took a few more sips of her cold drink and before getting up from the table again she added:

"I'd like you to buy me one of those big combs in the other shop."

"They're made of tortoise shell," Luis explained and when he had bought it, she tucked it between her shorts and her skin leaving part of it sticking out as though it were a knife handle, without trying it in her black hair, as Luis would have liked to see her do.

That night, after Katina and he had gone swimming again as their parents sat watching on the porch and talking, Katina came down to dinner in the same pair of white shorts and yellow bra top, and when dinner was over, as their parents sat down to a game of bridge, she asked him to come for another walk.

"Let's go to the cemetery," Luis suggested once they were outside.

"No. What for?" Katina answered in surprise. "I'd be scared."

"Of course you wouldn't," Luis persisted. "It's not like other cemeteries; it's close by and it hasn't been used for a long time now. But sometimes there are will-o'-the-wisps. I've seen them."

"What are they?" Katina asked.

"You'll see, well, if we're lucky. Come on," Luis answered all excited.

She hesitantly allowed him to take her there. The cemetery looked like an ordinary empty lot between one of the summer houses and a group of straw huts back of the highway, but it had a huge almond tree on one side. The two of them halted for a moment in front of the broken-down picket fence symbolically closing off the plot of ground, surrounded by three tiers of barbed wire. In the shadow of the almond tree, which cast the place in greater darkness still, it was nearly impossible to make out the outlines of the graves.

"It doesn't look like a cemetery," Katina said more confidently.

"I told you so. . ." Luis said and guided her inside, though he too was a little afraid and had made the comment in a low voice.

There was sand covering the narrow foot paths and even part of the gravestones, so that, had it not been for a few tumble-down crosses that stood out as they walked a little farther on inside, it would have felt as though they were walking on the beach. Katina and Luis headed for the almond tree, whose vast crown was like a reference point. Overhead, the sky with its blanket of stars stretched out to infinity, not like a vault, but like a limitless opening into which all possibility of a beyond disappeared. The smell of the sea reached them, intense and penetrating, along with its continuous murmur, whose rhythm changed with the motion of the waves. However, both of them, at the very same time, had the sensation that they had unexpectedly left everything far behind without intending to and that action brought them so close together that it turned them into a single person, so that one depended on the other to feel a sense of self. Beneath the shadow of the almond tree, Katina's black hair blended with the night. Her slender hand sought Luis's. He felt the touch of her fingers on his palm, yet she did not quite complete the movement, but kept herself apart, as though suddenly that contact with him, from the moment of their union, were unnecessary.

"Tell me, what you mean by that business about will-o'-the-wisps?" Katina asked him again.

"They're little flames that come out above the graves, as though there were a candle inside. They say it's on account of the phosphorus," he explained to her this time.

"Really?" she said excitedly, with a sudden interest in which there was not the least shadow of fear. "Have you seen them?"

"Sure," Luis said. "All it takes is enough dryness in the air."

But, really, he had only heard some of his older cousins talk of them and on one occasion he had vainly waited there on the spot with one of his friends for them to appear, the two of them containing their urge to take to their heels without either daring to confess it, and in previous years the temptation to go to the graveyard haunted almost the entire group of boys his age all through the two months of light and sea that constituted summer vacation, though the plan was almost never carried through, and yet many firmly maintained that they had been witness to the appearance of the will-o'-the-wisps. However, this time, a small flame began to move about one of the graves, as though it were coming from the tombstone, but a few centimeters above it, and almost at the same time, farther on, two others appeared. Their tiny glow seemed to envelop all the darkness of the night. Luis and Katina stood stock-still for a long time, their eyes fixed on the flames, as though the timid flickers, at each moment just about to disappear, were bright shining stars that their attention alone kept alive.

"Let's go over to them!" Luis finally said excitedly. "People say they follow you."

"No, wait," Katina answered, holding him back, too astonished to note that he had given away the lie he'd told before by making it plain that this was the first time that he too had seen the will-o'-the-wisps, and then she added in a very soft voice: "It's so pretty . . . ."

Luis realized then that neither of them was afraid. The timid fires born of the dead were really a form of life that their will seemed to have summoned forth, uniting naturally with the murmur of the night created by the sea and repeated in small by the distant twinkling of the stars in the open sky. In her amazement, Katina seemed more innocent and more of a little girl than ever and he instinctively put his arm round her bare shoulders, drawing her to him, so that she ended up leaning against his chest, without looking at him and without his being fully aware of her secret closeness and of the gentleness of the light weight of her body against his.

Then the flame that was just barely moving above the nearest grave vanished in the darkness as suddenly as it had appeared and immediately the one farthest away disappeared too; but the last one lingered still and even darted from one grave to another, as though it were playing, and for an instant they both felt at once, without having to tell each other so, that it would come over to their double figure, which now became even more closely united beneath the sheltering crown of the almond tree; however, following this tentative movement, the last little flame sank in the dark too. Luis and Katina remained silent for a long moment still, not moving, yet not knowing what they were waiting for either, till she turned her face toward him, her gaze seeking his in the darkness and said:

"What a pity! It was all over so soon."

Above her words, the murmur of the sea reached them with unexpected force and the two of them suddenly understood that it was useless to go on waiting. Luis removed his arm from her shoulders and they walked to the exit in silence. Only when they were out on the highway once again did Katina comment:

"I won't ever forget, Dwig. I didn't know that things like that happened. It's nice to be with you."

And in the beginning her voice had a grave accent, but the last sentence held her usual exultant joy.

They ran all the way back to the house along the shore, despite the fact that the loose sand made it heavy going to run, and as they came in all out of breath, Luis's mother looked up from the bridge game for a moment to ask them where they'd been, but before he'd finished telling her, Katina had already begun jabbering away excitedly with her parents in German, not even stopping to catch her breath and he had to wait for her to finish what sounded to him like a single long, harsh, and suddenly gentle word, before her father, after answering her, addressed Luis's parents in English and his father asked him where he'd gotten the idea of going to the cemetery.

"I go there all the time," Luis said, covered with confusion.

"Fibber!" his mother said with a smile; but Katina went on looking at him with an admiration such that her father drew her to him and said something in her ear which prompted her to push him away in a fury.

Then they sent them upstairs to bed. Katina's mother went up to her room with her, but Luis nonetheless had her to himself all the following morning. Katina appeared in a bathing suit as tiny as the red one, but a blue one this time, after he had already finished breakfast and been waiting, in a bathing suit too, an interminable time for her. She ate her breakfast almost without bothering to sit down, eager to get outside, without his being able to take his eyes off her slender figure, with slightly sunburned skin, getting to her feet again and again in a continual attempt, frustrated by hunger, to leave the table, washing down with swallows of coffee with milk the enormous chunks of bread she bit off, and once they were out on the beach she asked him to take her to the cemetery again.

"By day it's nothing," Luis said.

But she insisted and they went as far as the tumble-down fence, though, as a matter of fact, in the steady light of the sun the cemetery merely looked like a vacant lot half buried in sand, with a few bleached crosses, and the only striking thing was the shady, verdant beauty of the broad tapering crown of the almond tree, planted off to one side like an inexplicable living monument, so that Katina, as though she had forgotten all about the night's experience and now wanted only to assert her presence in the face of the motionless reality of the burning light of day, lost interest and turned round toward the sea, which dawn had found calmer and its waters much clearer than the day before.

In the afternoon, the others began to arrive. All of them were young people with whom Luis had shared his summers and certain memories up until then, but now their presence was a disturbing and unwelcome invasion of the pure instant, timeless and spaceless, that the days in Katina's company had become. It was they who were the strangers, his friends and his girl cousins and their girlfriends and their own cousins, all those who came and went from one house to another, including his own, as though the houses were an extension of the beach and belonged to each and all alike, so that in the entire town all possible privacy was lost in the name of a collective state of mind that, from a time long before Luis had begun to share it consciously, was part of summer and made it something special. From the terrace of his house, lying with Katina in the triangle of shadow cast by the wall on the mosaic tiles, which the two of them had chosen as their very own place since the afternoon on which, in the face of Katina's indifference, Luis had looked with her at the atlas in which it was so easy to fit their pasts together, the two now saw his earliest acquaintances calling to him from the beach, shouting to him to come down and join them.

"Who are they?" Katina had asked.

"Friends," Luis answered vaguely, aware already that very soon it was going to be impossible to avoid them and realizing, without being able to imagine the nearly continuous unrelieved irritation that awaited him, that he wanted to keep Katina all to himself.

And she kept herself for him, but in a way that, despite the fact that it was often apparent and Katina did her best to make it even more evident, he could not accept, unable to feel that it was enough for him after the first days of being by themselves, because what had changed was the very nature of their relationship, ceasing to be spontaneous and instead now requiring a deliberateness that, to Luis's despair, no matter how profoundly determined Katina was to make him see that she was still with him in the same way as in the beginning, merely seemed to emphasize the coyness that made her so attractive to others. And without realizing that what he was searching for and wanted and needed was not that Katina should show that she preferred him or even that she was his, but that she should be as independent and free as the first days, as self-possessed as the sea and the beach and the palms or the abandoned cemetery to which they did not return.

It was a slow but inevitable transformation and for that very reason a more painful one. On the same night that the adjoining houses also began to be all lighted up, his parents and Katina's had dinner with an aunt and uncle of Luis's and his two girl cousins came with them. More than the boys or at least to the same degree in the case of some of them, it was the girls whose curiosity and interest Katina aroused, vying for her company and making it more difficult for Luis to be near her, because up until then the groups of youngsters, as was no longer true of the ones who were older now, always split in two, and seeking out the company of girls was a sign that never went unnoticed among the others and one that all of them did their best to ward off with sneering jokes and snide remarks, as though they did not want the homogeneity of the group to be disturbed. And in this respect

Katina seemed to be no different from the others, merely disappearing with gay abandon among her new girlfriends until she became unattainable to Luis, who could only watch her from a distance, continually hoping for a sign of recognition that at times was never forthcoming or, on the contrary, was so obvious that he was obliged to pretend, to those who had hitherto been his boon companions, that it was of no importance. And yet, in such circumstances, Katina was even more present and more real than during those first days, now over and gone, in which the two had appeared to form, so simply and naturally, a new unity.

Katina would come out of the water immediately to catch up with him when he went walking along the shore with one or another of his friends, to oblige him to stop and place his leg alongside hers so as to leave their footprints on the wet sand.

"You see?" she would say. "They're the same size."

And the two of them would stand there next to each other, studying the similar footprints as his pals waited, looking at them without understanding what was going on, till a wave stronger than the ones before erased the outline of the footprints.

"It doesn't matter," Katina would add. "We already know they're just the same."

But one of her new girlfriends was there alongside her as well and the two were obliged to separate.

Later on, however, with some of the parents of these same girlfriends and of friends of his, a large part of the group, too numerous for the two cars available, would go, in the late afternoon, after the grownups had taken their siesta, to one of the nearby fishing villages, via the highway that ran almost along the shoreline. He and Katina, who had not paid sufficient attention to the time when they would be leaving, suddenly found themselves in different cars, but once they stopped, scattering along the beach, walking along the little roughhewn piers with wooden pylons and planks, lapped softly, rhythmically by the continuous ebb and flow of the sea, the two sought each other out, with the frank need that during the entire trip had made them await only the moment when they would be together again, and when it came time to go back, as they climbed into the cars, ignoring the confusion they caused, Luis managed to get a place next to Katina. Squeezed in with four or five other boys in the back seat, he was aware only that Katina's shoulder was resting against his chest and his left leg carefully shifting position so as to keep touching her right one each time it moved, as the last afternoon light faded round them, leaving them in intimate secret contact in the semi-darkness, aware only of that contact and enveloped by the penetrating smell of the salt air blowing in through the open window of the car, ruffling Katina's soft hair which every so often she pushed away from her face, ending the gesture each time with a slight pressure of one arm against Luis's chest.

They likewise all went together to spend the day, always with one or two pairs of parents to keep an eye on them, to one of the isolated beaches where the surf was stronger. Katina made herself more inaccessible then, disappearing from sight among all the other girls, as meanwhile he was obliged to show a certain loyalty to the group of males. But then they tried to set afloat once again a huge tree trunk that the waves had washed up on the beach. Only half paying attention to the task, unconsciously searching about for Katina's red-bikini-clad figure, Luis got a long narrow scratch from one of the sharp ends left by the broken-off branches of the slippery trunk when he failed to notice that they had already managed to get it into the water again and the waves were rocking it from side to side. Immediately, Katina was at his side, as concerned as though it were a really serious wound, using her hand to wipe away the blood that kept flowing and then instinctively wiping it off on her own legs, so that both of them had to get into the water together to really get clean. Later on, Katina sat down beside him at lunch time, ate half a sandwich and gave the rest of it to Luis, drank half a soft drink and passed the bottle to him, her blue eyes meeting Luis's for a fleeting instant or allowing his hand to linger for a long moment on hers as he took the bottle of soda.

"Halves on everything," she said very fast, almost not daring to smile.

And in those few quick words, in that mere hint of a smile, the weight of everyone else was apparent to Luis, making it all the more necessary to get her alone, leading him to doubt the truth of what she said, in a way that at times, all of a sudden, Katina seemed bent on making more profound.

She would come out of her room, at night, opening the door just as he was about to enter his own on returning from the house of one of his friends.

"Have you been to the cemetery?" she would ask him.

88

"No," he said. "I'll only go back there with you, I promise. And what have you been up to?"

Katina was already dressed for bed, in a nightgown closed all the way up the front to her neck but without sleeves and baring her legs completely, accentuating the definite tan color her skin had taken on and making her eyes bluer still, and beneath his gaze it took her a moment to answer:

"Nothing. I had dinner at your girl cousins' and afterwards they all started talking about you boys."

"And what did you say?" Luis dared to ask.

"Not a word," Katina answered and to his even greater happiness she added: "Let's go out to the terrace."

They then stretched out on the floor again, with their backs against the wall, below her bedroom window, listening to the murmur of the sea, not knowing what to say to each other, till Luis, unable to keep to himself the terrible melancholy whose origin he was not interested in explaining to himself, worked up his courage to remark:

"I liked it better when we were alone."

Katina allowed an interminable moment to go by during which even the breaking of the waves seemed to stop.

"I think my mom and dad feel that way too," slipping away then, for no reason, for the sheer pleasure of the game perhaps, but definitely keeping him, full of fury now, from trying to say more.

That same fury, which made him want to go off by himself forever, reappeared when the two opposite but parallel sides of the group mingled as they swam out to the same motorboat or gathered under the same sun umbrella and Luis saw that some friend of his was helping Katina aboard, receiving the same look she sometimes gave him, or she was talking with another, recounting to him things about her life in Germany that she had not told him. Thus, at the house of one of the girls, in the living room opening onto the beach where six or seven of them had come in to have a cool drink with the same freedom with which they all entered any of the houses known to them, still soaking wet and leaving the sand on their feet all over the floor, he heard her answer, when questioned by one of them as to why she had black hair if her parents were blond, that her grandmother had been born in Brazil of a German mother and a Brazilian father, at the same time tossing that black hair forward so that it would fall over her shoulders to either side of her neck and Luis felt that it was an insult for her to satisfy others' curiosity by giving out with something he did not yet know. Then, as the two of them were eating with their parents, he suddenly asked her, after having kept silent the whole time, as though the query had come from deep down inside and been hard for him to come out with:

"And where is she now?"

Katina looked at him questioningly, not understanding what he was talking about.

"Who?" she said then.

Luis's mother, listening to the conversation, looked at him too, and he turned red in the face, thinking that perhaps he hadn't really understood Katina's explanation because during it he had pretended not to be listening, and he added haltingly:

"Your grandmother, the Brazilian. . . ."

"Oh, her . . ." Katina said. "She's in München; she lives with one of my aunts. But she's not Brazilian. She just lived there for a year. She doesn't even speak Brazilian."

"Portuguese; in Brazil they speak Portuguese," Luis corrected her peevishly, increasingly aware that his mother was listening to every word.

"It's all the same to me. Such things don't interest me. You understand me, don't you?"

"Who knows," Luis said and felt obliged to pursue the subject in order to prove that he had logic on his side and, obscurely, to annoy her. "And your great-grandfather?"

"He died the year my grandmother was born. So they went back to Germany. The whole thing is so mixed up; I don't know anything about all that," Katina answered.

"You're pestering her, Luis. Don't ask her any more questions," his mother spoke up then.

"No, I'm not pestering her," Luis said; but he didn't say another word during the meal and avoided both his mother's eye and Katina's, concentrating all his attention on his plate, certain that his mother was talking about him in English with her father and mother.

When he'd finished eating, he left the table before anyone else and shut himself up in his room, furious and ashamed, with his fury adding fuel to his shame and shame feeding his fury. A moment later, Katina knocked at his door. She was still wearing the red bikini she had eaten lunch in, with the straps of the top untied and dangling down, and was combing her hair with the comb that he had given her as a present.

"Why did you get angry?" she said the moment he opened the door, entering the room as she continued to drag the comb through her long tangled hair.

"I'm not angry," Luis said, not hiding his scorn.

She looked at him for an instant, searching his eyes with all the dark depth of her blue gaze, still combing her hair, and then gave him a quick kiss on the cheek.

Without realizing what he was doing, instead of allowing her to leave, Luis took her by the wrist and drew her to him. She put up no resistance and then he held her in a close embrace, feeling in his hands, as though through them he recognized the taste of the sea and something that resembled nothing, that was superior to everything and was Katina's skin, her slender back and the strap of her bikini, as his legs clung to hers. Then he sought her mouth till he found, first passing over her hair slightly stiffened by salt water, her thin lips, very dry at that moment, which, although she had not answered his embrace but, rather, allowed herself to be embraced with her arms at her sides and the comb in her hand still, opened at the touch of his and the freshness of her moist tongue entered his mouth, till the lips of both were wet as well and Luis, receiving her tongue or placing his in her mouth, felt that they would never come to an end, but would remain as they were forever, thinking of nothing, with their two bodies now made one by way of their mouths. Katina, however, at no moment raised her arms to answer Luis's embrace and finally drew her lips away and hid her head in his neck, without freeing herself from his embrace, as though incapable of further motion.

"Have you been kissed before?" Luis asked, not

thinking of what he was saying, from out of the absence of himself in which the nearness of her had submerged him.

"Yes," she answered and an instant later, incapable still of removing her face from its refuge in his neck, she added: "But I don't like it."

Only then did she draw away, as though she were slipping out of his hands, his embrace, and Luis could see her a few paces away from the body that he was incapable of feeling as his own, lost in that boundless emptiness from which it seemed to be impossible to return to the reality of the room, incredibly close and far away in her tiny red bikini, with her long slender arms and legs, as golden brown from the sun as her belly and her face, with her black hair falling forward over just one of her shoulders this time and her blue eyes opened wide, looking not at him but beyond him, through him, suddenly untouchable and, nonetheless, present in such a way that there existed nothing but her and round about her, given the disappearance of all solid bodies, there was only light.

Katina looked at him without seeing him, as though she sought in him something she could not find, but of which he alone could possibly be the depositary, thus condemning her to go on searching for him and only in him, and then she said:

"I asked my father. My great-grandfather was half-German too, but his name was da Silva."

Then, before Luis had time to answer, as though knowing that it was impossible for him to say anything, she left the room.

There were still almost three weeks left before the end of the two traditional months of vacation. The sea was so calm and transparent that it seemed to exist only so that the light would play over the sandy white bottom setting it in motion as it traveled toward the beach in obedience to the delicate rhythm of the waves, and the sky was a sheer dazzling emptiness, without a single shadow, in which the eye found it impossible to make out even the sun, for it too was hiding, behind its own light. Meanwhile, after that one kiss, the unity of Luis and Katina appeared to have entered another dimension, without their will having intervened or been capable of changing it. They were closer to each other, but in a secret way now, so that on turning Katina into something impenetrable Luis felt her to be farther away than ever, though nonetheless, again and again, seemingly at the limit which would lead her to open herself forever, but without his knowing how to go beyond that limit, as the fury that would suddenly overcome him interposed itself between him and his own desires. Katina pretended that everything was still the same and out of weariness Luis, at times, adopted the same attitude; but nothing was true. And now, moreover, when there were more intruders than ever, the presence of the others, his own need for the nearness of Katina, for the contact with the skin and lips of Katina, for the surrender of Katina, would appear to be an attribute of them as well, or one that, at any rate, he ascribed to them, without his being interested in getting to the bottom of which of the two things was the truth of the matter, was more intolerable than ever and resulted in his being torn between an inevitable loyalty to the memory of so many past summers that obliged him to feel them to be his

94

friends, part and reality of his own world, and the irrepressible desire to see the last of them disappear, leaving him with Katina, free together in that pure spaceless center which they had created between the two of them.

They held mock tournaments in the water. Two girls would climb up onto the backs of two boys, with their thighs around their waists, as they in turn held them firmly in place atop their bodies with their hands, and each rider tried to unhorse her opponent, doing her best to hold her under water till she was forced to let go of the boy playing the part of her mount. Very often the contest was such an even match that it went on endlessly. The couples approached each other and drew apart, circled one about the other, engaged each other by pulling on the opponent, with the enemy managing to escape thanks to the skill of the mount or the rider's ability to stay under water, as her horse tried to retreat when all appeared to be lost, and then, with a joyous burst of triumphant laughter, tried in her turn to be the one to get the upper hand on attacking; and very often Luis was Katina's mount and Katina Luis's rider. The attention that had to be concentrated on the fight then mingled with the keen consciousness and the disturbing pleasure that accompanied it of having his hands round Katina's delicious legs and her body clinging to his back, as one of her arms twined round his neck, holding him so tightly in the difficult moments of the fight that it almost hurt him and her laughter and her gasps echoed behind him, and all this made him feel her closeness, the pleasure of each one of the contacts of her body with his, with such intensity that the immediate goal of the game was completely lost from sight in the fog of his emotions, though he did not leave off executing with all the skill of which he was capable each one of the actions that the battle required, as within himself he never even for a moment ceased to wonder to what point her sensations of this union of their bodies were exactly like his own and which of all the most powerful contacts and pressures, besides being provoked by the demands of the game, might also be evidence of the intention, on her part, of enhancing that union, until the double unit formed by himself and Katina emerged as the winner, or, what was perhaps more agreeable still, saw itself obliged to dissolve its embrace in the confusion that the triumph of its opponents created for them under water, so that both Katina and he appeared to want to prolong that embrace beyond all possibility, beyond the limits that the need to return to the surface imposed on them, despite the fact that, once more, many times, Katina again put her arms about his neck and embraced him, but from the front now, laughing happily, as though defeat were also a victory, and with his wet body clinging to hers, feeling her slender arms round his neck, he was unable to explain to himself when the impulse to lose himself forever in this embrace was interrupted and he suddenly found himself far from her again, separated now and in empty space. But then too, on many other occasions, after these moments of absolute unawareness amid happiness, Katina immediately climbed on another boy's back and whether it was his turn to be the enemy or whether he simply watched the fight as a spectator, Luis, suffering from a total despair and impotence owing to the impossi-

bility of his knowing to what point his fears that
Katina adopted the same attitudes with the others as
with him and the other was receiving at this moment
the same secret pressures, the same deliberately sought
contacts that he thought he perceived when he had her
joined as one to his back, found himself carried away
in the opposite direction, focusing completely on his
separation from Katina and his loneliness, with so
impenetrable an ignorance of the true character of his
feelings and his sensations that, amid raging fury and
his impotent self-reproaches for the possible, and
fervently hoped-for, injustice of his suspicions, the
immediate reality of the actions and even of the world
around him vanished for him. And this state of mind
was repeated on the most unexpected occasions for the
least predictable apparent reasons. At times it sufficed
for him to water-ski close in to shore and on turning
round toward the beach catch just a glimpse of Katina
conversing beneath the shade of a sun umbrella with
one or another of his old friends or, suddenly, as she
swam out to one of the motorboats anchored just
offshore, for one of them to follow her and the two of
them end up climbing into the boat together, as Luis
struggled between his desire to join them and his
determination to remain apart and have Katina be the
one to approach him, although he also could not help
thinking that perhaps she wanted him to be there, at
her side, in that unreachable boat, and then his rage
was directed against his inability to go through with
the apparently easy and natural movement that would
place him alongside her and perhaps even give him
the satisfaction, in anticipation so difficult and
miraculous and in attainment so natural as to be

incommunicable, of asking her, as on so many other occasions, to dive into the sea again together, whereupon he would suddenly thrust his head up out of the water to find Katina's a few yards away, framed by her black hair with the tips of her long eyelashes and the perfect arch of her eyebrows sparkling with drops of water, or would wait for her to appear at that point in which the sea found its entire truth through her presence. But perhaps the worst moments, the most uncertain, the most terrible and the most enjoyable ones after that first and only kiss that now seemed almost to have been dreamed in its unreal reality, presented themselves when the two of them were alone. It was late in the afternoon and Katina was on the upstairs terrace in a light dress, the breeze stirring the skirt of it and her black hair alike or in shorts and one of her sleeveless blouses or even in one of her minuscule bathing suits still, to him so different from those of all the other girls, leaning over the railing with her elbows resting on the edge, her arms stretched out in front of her and her hands intertwined, motionless between the light growing softer and softer and the breeze, like a living statue holding within its mysterious fragility all the beauty of the world round about her, as her blue eyes were lost in contemplation of the endless ever-changing expanse of the sea, watching how the sun lingered on the horizon, no less unreachable than herself, and Luis, who from his room had seen her appear and halt in the precise spot at which his gaze could take in all of her through the window frame, came outside and stood just behind her, not quite touching her, but so close that her hair ruffled by the breeze suddenly brushed his face, and as

Katina ignored or pretended to ignore his presence, it felt to him as though he were touching the closeness of her body, overcoming the impulse to embrace her without being able to explain to himself why, breathing in her odor, certain at times that in her immobility she was acceding to his closeness and her body containing and controlling the same tension as his own, till Katina turned round, bringing her face so close to Luis's that her features became a blur and said:

"Look at the sun before it goes down."

Or simply:

"Dwig, I didn't know you were there behind me; come and sit here."

He then would imitate her position and her bare arm was joined to his from the tip of her intertwined hands to her shoulder, though without the contact ceasing to appear accidental, just as it might appear that their shoulders merely chanced to touch continually as they walked along the seashore or the highway at night, returning from the house of one of his friends among the boys or hers among the girls or relatives of Luis's who were now hers too, alone at last, though the only thing that happened was that Luis would enter that different terrain of doubts that being alone created, thinking, even if he were speaking at the same time of some nonsense or other, that she had said that she had been kissed before but didn't like it, with no way of knowing if this failure to like the experience included his kiss, until they arrived home and after kissing their parents and saying goodnight to the visitors if there were any, in accordance with the custom that Katina had introduced, they went upstairs to their rooms and in the eternal instant that preceded the separation till the following day, which to Luis always seemed to be the last one they had left, Katina looked into his eyes and he looked into Katina's, certain that she would fling herself into his arms, only to find, rather, that all she did was make her way at last out of the void surrounding them with a quick "See you in the morning."

Nonetheless, whenever he sought to make his interest and his need for her evident by carefully keeping his distance, Katina invariably used all her free-and-easy naturalness to draw him to her side again, as though in her there existed no conflict and they simply had to be together because that was how it had been with them from the beginning. That was her way of approaching him even when he was alone with his friends and no female was with them and in drawing closer in this way at no time did she conceal her desire to be with Luis, with Luis alone among all of them; but within his happiness at such times there was no possibility of intimacy, precisely because Katina did everything in such a direct way, so open to a natural abandonment of self that it was not a surrender of self because it seemed to antedate them, turning them into a sort of brother and sister or something even more than brother and sister, the reflection of a single figure that had suddenly become double, the one thing about it that might be cause for surprise being a difference within its oneness. And so she would fling herself on his back, putting her arms around his neck as when they were playing in the water, or take him by the arm and walk alongside him keeping in step with him, leaning her head on his shoulder in such a way that her hair lay over his mouth and Luis breathed in together with the salt air the incomparable fragrance of that pure and all-enveloping black mystery, only to, immediately, go off in search of something or obey the summons of one of those who were again his friends but for that very reason more intrusive than ever. Then he was left with the echo of her closeness constituting so powerful a presence that Katina appeared to have gone off without leaving him and he continued to feel the weight of her body next to his, on his, as his eyes carefully watched the ever-changing pattern that Katina's figure was not leaving in space but, miraculously, drawing back wholly into itself, as though all her movements, very often so rapid and nervous, so rash and so outwardly meaningless, were part of a single image, foreign to time and space, that inevitably found its own equilibrium in the inapprehensible beauty of each one of its parts, centered on a given instant which vanished into the one that followed before reaching the point of becoming concrete and which was formed of the limpid and inexplicable sound of her laughter, or the deep, grave note with which one or another of her continuous exclamations of enthusiasm, surprise, or joy defined the range of her voice, a child's still and yet absolutely personal, her very own, or the tilt of her face to one side, emphasizing the endless curve of her neck, whose skin, beneath which the veins played, seemed barely to cover it before blending into the line of her shoulders, or the movement of her long legs and her slender arms, whose changes of position gave them every appearance of always being parallel even if they performed actions through which it appeared impossible to discover the reason for their obeying a single impulse, born of the indestructible totality of her as a figure, that totality of which the sum of her facial features, with the deep yet gentle hollow of the cheeks beneath the prominent cheek bones, the arch of the eyebrows opening up and accenting the rectilinearity of the broad forehead, the only slightly angular outline of the chin and, in the center, the blue eyes forever staring in wonder and amazement, the straight nose and the thin mouth anticipating for some unfathomable reason the possibility of a smile, was evidence of a perfection of which, to Luis's amazement, she never appeared to be conscious, not even when her acts made him think that she was offering him the whole of it, nor when, without anything having changed outwardly, she appeared to be an unreachable distance away, making herself as remote in her deceptive retreat as the line of the horizon, which in reality marked neither the end nor the beginning of anything.

In like manner, when she was at Luis's, as they were waiting to sit down at the table or their parents were coming downstairs after their siesta, with a shamelessness that very often embarrassed him, forcing him to ask himself whether behind Katina's actions there did not lie the hidden intention of making him appear ridiculous in the eyes of the parents of both of them, she, whose figure he was unable to tear his eyes from, as though the entire reality of the house was sustained thanks only to her presence, carried to an extreme, which up until then Luis had thought unimaginable, her demonstrations of affection for her father, seating herself on his lap in her minuscule bathing suit, speaking almost in his ear in German, laughing with a strange complicity, fondly ruffling his blond hair as she showered him with kisses on the cheeks, the neck, the chest, till her father, with an exclamation incomprehensible to Luis, though from the tone it must have been at once one of affection and rejection, rose to his feet with her in his arms, lifting her up bodily and immediately setting her down on the floor, as one puts an animal down when its proofs of affection are at once pleasing and bothersome, whereupon Katina would head straight to Luis, who had been pretending to look the other way or was hiding his interest behind the unfolded pages of a newspaper, and suddenly thrusting the paper aside or announcing her arrival with a little outcry, would alight on his lap in exactly the same way, as the parents of the two of them looked on with a smile, leaning her head on his shoulder as on so many occasions in the presence of Luis's friends and compelling him, by resorting to the simple device of taking his arms and guiding their movements, to embrace her, looking with a smile of false scorn at the parents who were talking in English, of them no doubt, Luis thought, and saying in a very loud voice: "We don't need them, right?" without Luis's being able, completely divided as he was into two contradictory parts by embarrassment and pleasure, to get a single word out, though the look which was meant to be one of complicity with his parents and proved to be beyond his ability to interpret made him feel that he ought to discover powers that would allow him to laugh too and treat Katina with the apparently rough affection with which he had just seen her father deal with her. Then it was Katina who drew away, getting up off his legs with the same naturalness with which she had permitted her incredible weight to rest in his lap, fusing her skin with his in a single contact, and the sudden absence of that contact with his skin, of that weight on his legs, feather-light at the moment when he had it on top of him and intolerable once it was gone, was superior to any embarrassment he might experience and quite enough to make the presence of the parents disappear completely.

But thus hanging suspended in the loftiest fascination, during those last weeks in which people, everybody else, the others, were beginning to straggle back to the city, so that more and more of the summer houses again stood shuttered and silent, Luis, apart from those who were still enjoying the sea, the beach, and the all-embracing light that formed part of themselves, could not help feeling, though unable even to think of this existence as necessarily having an end, that his growing exasperation and the abrupt breaks between the most absolute union and the most inexplicable separation with Katina kept him in a state that each day proved farther beyond his possibilities of understanding and controlling, giving rise to the most unexpected attacks of fury and uncertainty, of fury born of uncertainty and of uncertainty provoked by the inexplicable unreasonableness of his fury. Prisoner of this state, his one consolation the knowledge that Katina and her parents would be staying on in the house for a time whose limit had not been fixed, thus allowing him to consider it simply endless for the very same reason that kept him from recalling that a period prior to their arrival existed or should exist in his memory, he finally reached the moment, desired at most times, with the exception of the occasions on which Katina made a show of being one and the same person with him in front of others, and at other times feared, without his being able to discover the reason for this fear, when, with the exception of a few who could be regarded as mere acquaintances and therefore didn't count, all his friends had already gone back to the city. The afternoon of that day was marked by farewells and the steady sound of cars going by on the highway. That evening, Luis and Katina were invited to dinner at the house of the cousins who, on a day that already seemed incredibly distant, had invaded his house. From the beginning Katina and these cousins had established a sort of feminine complicity between them that made Luis feel set apart, left out, and a bit ridiculous, almost making him think with nostalgia of the company of his friends. All of a sudden, without ceasing to be present in Luis's continuous admiration, at that moment which should have marked the hoped-for return to their dual solitude, Katina turned out to be farther away than ever, stooping so low as to become a figure indistinguishable from his cousins, making herself their equal. Then, after dinner was over, the cousins found an excuse to go up to their room instead of everybody going for a walk along the beach as Luis had proposed. He found that as a male it was impossible for him to go upstairs with them to have a look at some dumb thing like clothes that could only interest females and said crossly that he would wait for them on the porch, despite the sudden intensity with which Katina's blue eyes riveted for an instant on his seemed to ask him to come upstairs.

His cousins' parents had gone in turn to his house for dinner and Luis went out onto the porch more furious still because Katina's look seemed as usual to hold the promise of a happiness that was never fulfilled. He sat down, surrounded by darkness, in one of the rocking chairs on the porch, making it, without his realizing it, sway back and forth in time to the marked rhythm of the movement of the sea, which reached him with complete clarity from out of the absence of a space impossible to determine, and he allowed what seemed to him an interminable time to go by, during which he felt more and more lonely, hurt and angry, full of an inexplicable nostalgia for his past prior to meeting Katina, until, impetuously, guided by a rage whose one target was Katina and yet was not aimed at her concrete person, but at something that encompassed her and at one and the same time was part of her and outside of her, he got up from the rocking chair and left the house without a word to anyone, walking along the shore to his house, furious with himself as well now for having taken this first step, yet unable to turn back. Then, that past for which a moment before he had thought he felt nostalgia and of which he had spoken to Katina on the first night, sitting together on the porch steps at his house, proved to be something unbearable as well, as he sensed that if she no longer belonged to him he had nothing and was intolerably alone, surrounded by feelings, thoughts, murmurs he could not make out, in the darkness detached from space in which the night was passing and amid which he was walking.

When he entered his house, completely withdrawn into his own fury, as if this were the one reality capable of reaching him, his parents were still at the table with their guests.

"Where's Katina?" his mother asked him.

"She stayed behind with the cousins," he said and bade everyone goodnight and went upstairs to his room almost without looking toward the dining room, avoiding any possible further questioning.

In his room he began aimlessly rummaging about among his clothes and the favorite objects that had accumulated in the closet over the years and been left there forgotten between one summer and another. Then he stood next to his bed for a long time, stock-still, listening to the sound of the sea and overcoming the impulse to go out onto the terrace, and finally he got undressed, turned out the light and threw himself on the bed, lying in the dark with his eyes open, unable even to feel his rage now, though it enveloped him completely, until he thought he heard Katina's voice in the living room and then distinctly made out her footsteps on the stairs and sensed how they stopped for an endless moment in the hallway, being certain that it was impossible for him to move toward her, and then, the moment after that, calming him almost by opening a new pause in the tension of waiting, the door of her room opened and closed, shutting her up safely inside.

In the morning, on awakening, he still felt the same dull rage turning back against him while at the same time it struck him as the product of Katina's aloofness, an aloofness he immediately imagined to have been provoked by him, so that his unfocused rancor turned into an endless circle from which there was no escape. On that account perhaps, instead of immediately putting on his bathing suit to go downstairs and have breakfast as he had done since the second day that she had been in the house, he donned a pair of pants and a shirt and for no reason at all loaded the old shotgun that he had found among his things the night before and took it down to the dining room, consciously avoiding looking at the door of Katina's room as he left his. He had breakfast without noticing what he was eating, feeling the house to be oddly silent and too big round about him, as though he had suddenly found himself on the first day of an inexplicable time within which everything that, ever since he had had a memory and could recollect, had always been known to him was now alien and strange, and went down to sit on the beach, on the sand that was already beginning to be burning-hot, beneath the blindingly bright light that washed out the colors of the sea, toward which he was looking without seeing, allowing his sense of sight to lose itself in the absence of limits being born of the absolute union between that sea, now a sheer brightness, and the line of the horizon.

Then Katina had appeared, standing behind him. Luis recognized her presence as though the whole of it were weighing down upon his body, making him feel it to be more his than ever, traversed, made concrete, by a tension that was unbearable, yet at the same time kept him from turning round toward Katina.

"An woran denkst du?" Katina had at last said softly, in her grave tone of voice, speaking to him for the first time in German and thereby making him feel

that she was the Katina of the first day, whom he had looked at for a time without end as the parents of the two of them had conversed, not daring to speak to her, thinking that her wondrous beauty would always be untouchable.

"That means 'What are you thinking about?'" Katina added at once, in the same grave tone still, as he turned round to look at her, slowly eying her slender feet, which, as she had verified by the footprints in the wet sand, were the same size as his, the long legs that finally disappeared from sight in the brief blue shorts, the white blouse leaving her arms free and last of all the face framed by the black hair, on whose blue eyes his own lingered before he answered in a tone of voice ill-tempered still:

"Nothing. Nothing at all."

"Why?" she said, sitting down beside him.

"I don't know. I prefer to be by myself," Luis answered, and looked back out to sea.

Katina remained silent for a moment, she too looking toward the limitless horizon as though trying to see what he was seeing. All of a sudden, she seemed to have gone inside herself, becoming a grown-up, and yet she was the same Katina, at once delicate and determined, sure of herself and wondrously childlike still.

"Are you angry, Dwig?" she said then, turning round to look at him.

"No," he answered and the impossibility of telling the truth forced him to retreat even farther into that fury foreign to himself and unwanted.

"What do you want that rifle for?" Katina asked

then, as though she were unaware of what was going on inside him and they could converse normally.

"It's not a rifle. It's a shotgun," he said, almost scornfully. But then he felt compelled to add:

"I used to kill iguanas with it, and buzzards. But that was a long time ago."

"I see . . ." Katina said, not understanding.

"It was fun then. . . . But now everything's different," Luis said. He stood up and held his hand out to her. "Come on, let's walk."

"Where to?" Katina asked, raising her eyes to look at him, before allowing him to help her to her feet, entrusting her slender hand to his.

"Just walk. Along the beach, away from the houses," he answered.

And now, in fact, they had left everything behind and were walking along enveloped in the light with no need to talk, or to touch each other, followed only by the watchful seagull, not knowing when the moment would come to stop walking, with Luis showing no sign of his fury now, as though he had abandoned it, forgotten now, among the houses and without being fully conscious of it, felt only the nearness of Katina, which nonetheless was everything, the one reality amid the dazzling brightness; without knowing what she was expecting, though when Luis stopped for a moment to take off his shirt and tie it about his waist and roll up his pants legs, Katina felt with a terrible and wondrous force the need to embrace him and had been inexplicably obliged to contain her impulse only because of the sudden discovery of the seagull, suspended in its flight amid the burning emptiness of the sky, and now, the pure spaceless light that surrounded them, moving forward through time suspended in a single instant that was ever the same, within her was the fixed thought that in a moment whose arrival she could not imagine she would stop to take off her clothes and enter the sea, which would surely receive her as though it were the Luis who was walking untouchable at her side, the shotgun over his shoulder.

The line of bushes drained of color that blocked off the absence of space on the side opposite the sea only to leave an opening once again for the unattainable horizon had become thicker and higher as the thought fixed in some hidden part of Katina became an act and she unexpectedly sat down on the sand. Surprised, Luis too came to a halt, and lowered his eyes to look at her.

"What's the matter?" he asked.

"Nothing, as you say," she answered. "There's too much light. I can't see any more; I want to swim."

Luis stood at her side, not understanding. The seagull too had halted in its flight and was hovering in circles without overtaking them, with slow movements of its great white wings, creating its own, unique space, amid the infinite, luminous, empty immensity.

Without at any moment looking at Luis, as though suddenly completely unaware of his presence and only the sea existed for her, Katina unbuttoned her blouse, quickly ridding herself of it and, in like manner, her shorts. Luis had not really been able to see her as, in what seemed to him a single instant, she performed these acts; but immediately she rose to her feet.

111

"Aren't you coming?" she asked him, unhurried now.

Only then did he really notice that Katina was naked and so close that he had only to stretch out his hand to touch her. Yet he could neither move nor speak. The image of her was the same as when she appeared in one of her tiny bathing suits, but now, instead of a bit of red or blue cloth, her bathing suit was but a memory indicated by the lighter color of her skin in the places where ordinarily she kept it covered and he saw her little bare breasts with their unimaginable nipples, already a woman's, jutting out in the center, and beyond the lightest line of her skin, marking the beginning or the end of the vanished bathing suit, the black hair of her pubis, now an absolute reality. Otherwise, Katina was the same. Her hair fell over her familiar shoulders, her blue eyes were looking at him; but on her thin lips there was no smile; they were, rather, firmly pressed together, closed completely, unlike that body that was opening for the first time to him and had a new definitive center for all her beauty, a center resplendent in its blackness, as adorable and as distant as the little breasts which, with their nipples also bared, he was seeing for the first time though he had caught glimpses of them so many times before and been so embarrassed. And so, naked, Katina's body, the whole of Katina, lost all guile, all trace of the fascination that had worked its spell through her natural coyness, and was now more innocent and pure and unique than ever; but he was vanishing at her side.

In the face of his silence, she turned away and entered the sea. He saw how the waves, so delicate they barely broke against the beach with a slight crack, caressed her legs as they swirled round them, and saw her long slender back intersected by the clear line that pointed to the vanished presence of her bikini top, her hips only a little more pronounced than his own but beyond the shadow of a doubt already a woman's, the outline of the curve of her buttocks that so inexplicably blended into the long firmness of her legs and, farther up, the same inexhaustible black hair in which even the force of the light disappeared, turning into darkness. Thereupon the sea, until then so transparent, took on a dense new texture as Katina's figure vanished from sight within it. A moment later, her head and a fragment of her shoulders reappeared, more distant now, unreachable amid the water, and he looked at them, numbed by the force of his need to go to them, yet, for that very reason, unable to move, feeling how the fury that had so many times seized him in the months before mounted through his body till it filled his head, making him hate himself, but at the same time hate Katina even more, to the point that he could not go on looking at her. Then his eyes discovered the seagull, flying in broad circles, very slowly, almost directly above her head, making what up until that moment had been a pure emptiness with no possible contours turn into a heavy space, completely closed all round her. In a blind rage, not thinking of what he was doing, he took the shotgun from his shoulder and fired one single, terrible shot at the seagull.

Time, till then so nonexistent, seemed to begin spinning madly past at the sound of the shot and yet it was as though everything happened in a single instant. The seagull halted in its flight, remaining motionless for an eternity, as paralyzed as he himself had been in front of Katina a moment before; simultaneously, she gave a scream that appeared to be superimposed upon the sharp crack of the shot and before the sound of her voice died away, the seagull began to fall, as though its graceful lightness had suddenly turned into the dead weight of a stone.

Katina swam to the beach, raced out of the water, and ran past Luis as though he did not exist, not stopping in her frantic travel toward the point behind the line of bushes where the seagull's body had fallen. Instinctively, becoming himself again only then, from out of the seemingly irretrievable past in which she had appeared naked before his gaze, Luis followed her. Katina had now gone beyond the barrier of the bushes and was heading toward the body of the seagull, lying vanquished on the sand as white as itself with its vast extended wings stained by the red of its blood, its head doubled back onto its breast in a broken circle, when he managed to catch up with her and stopped her by seizing her by the waist. Katina writhed in his arms, straining to free herself and screaming broken words at him in a mixture of Spanish and German, which taken together gave voice to a single fury and desperation. Their bodies fused once again, as in the sea when they played at mock battles on horseback, but what united them now was one and the same impotent violence. Luis felt Katina's nails in his side and her teeth sank into his shoulder. Blinded with rage, yet unable to strike her, he flung her down onto the sand, where she went on writhing, possessed of a force until then unknown to him, weaving the wild black stain of her hair from side to side. He finally managed to immobilize her almost completely by stretching his body out on top of hers and holding her down by the wrists so that only her head continued to move rebelliously on the white sand, her uninterrupted outburst of words now silenced. Then Katina lay completely motionless and her blue eyes, independent of her panting breath, foreign to her vanquished body and her arms outspread in a cross, pinned to the sand by the hands holding her wrists down, opened to Luis. Dazed and stupefied, he looked at her without seeing her.

"Dwig . . ." Katina murmured.

Luis let go of her wrists and then his lips were on Katina's and he recognized her wet tongue and her hands, instead of scratching him, stroked his back, the two of them once again a double, single solitary figure, lying dirty with sand on the white sand, and suddenly he was inside Katina without her protesting even though Luis could feel the resistance of her body as he entered, only to lose himself immediately with her, in her, united in a shadowless space, independent of themselves, yet created by their limitless bodies, in the gentleness of an oblivion that had no end within its nature as an instant and that united them in the unlimited clarity of consciousness to which they gave birth out of their own darkness, isolating them from the world and delivering them over to the world.

Much later, her black hair was spread out over his chest and her parted lips silently pressed against the pulses of the vein in his neck. As the sole presence round about them in the emptiness that showed itself farther on, the light enveloped them like a delicate coverlet, its very warmth tenuous, able to prove its weight only by its contact with their bodies. Then, as though she had awakened from a lone dream to enter the day for the first time, Katina barely lifted her head, pushed aside the hair that covered part of her face and said almost in a whisper, her blue eyes riveted on his:

"Dwig, *die Möwe*, the seagull. . . ."

The two of them raised their heads and timidly looked about and then rose to their feet, unable to believe their eyes; but the seagull was no longer there.

The Eridanos Library

Eridanos Press, Inc., P.O. Box 211, Hygiene, CO 80533

This book was printed in February of 1989 by
Il Poligrafico Piemontese P.PM. in Casale Monferrato, Italy.
The Type is Baskerville 12/14.
The paper is Arcoprint 112 grs. for the insides
and Acquerello Bianco 160 grs. for the jacket,
both manufactured by Cartiera Fedrigoni, Verona,
especially for this collection.